In the Shadow Man's Lair

I struggled against an Arctic mass that had gathered force and held me captive.

I couldn't move.

"Mr. Madrix? Help me!"

The lights overhead abruptly wavered and went out. In the darkness everything seemed frightening. I was beginning to imagine the sound of bats squeaking overhead when I heard footsteps slowly walking down the stairs. Then I saw the welcoming glow of candle-light. The principal was coming to my rescue after all.

I began to breathe a sigh of relief until I saw who, or what, descended the stairs.

Shadow Man. A hooded and caped Shadow Man bearing a candle whose flickering glow made a mon-strous mask out of half-hidden features.

When the figure was ten steps from me, it stopped. It lowered the candle, pursed its lips and began to whistle. The hair at the back of my neck quivered to attention.

ELLEN LEROE

A MINSTREL® BOOK

PUBLISHED BY POCKET BOOKS

New York   London   Toronto   Sydney   Tokyo   Singapore

A MINSTREL PAPERBACK *ORIGINAL*

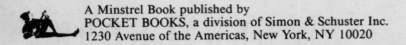 A Minstrel Book published by
POCKET BOOKS, a division of Simon & Schuster Inc.
1230 Avenue of the Americas, New York, NY 10020

ISBN: 0-671-68568-6

First Minstrel Books printing September 1991

10 9 8 7 6 5 4 3 2 1

A MINSTREL BOOK and colophon are registered trademarks
of Simon & Schuster Inc.

Cover art by Tom Stimson

Printed in the U.S.A.

*For Andy Bossi, the original Drac,
and Paul Herrerias, creative consultant:
Fangs for everything!*

1

No one had a better going-away party than I did. It was in honor of my transferring to a new school, nearly three thousand miles away. So it had to be special. And because my mother came from the wonderful, wacky, and magical Mandori family, it was.

First Aunt Tagoor's bridge club members—and fellow witches—had soared overhead on broomsticks in my honor.

Then Cousin Wa'albi, a Frankenstein's monster look-alike, had transformed a clear sunny September day into a thundery, rainy one—and back again in seconds just to amuse me.

My uncles, three-eyed trolls, followed these stunts by tap-dancing for me on the patio. Then, for a finale, they tapped up the side of the house to the wild cheers and applause of all my relatives.

Last but not least, my mother, Magdalena Mandori, a witch herself and no slouch in the spell department, carried in my five-layer farewell cake without touching it once with her hands.

Uncle Frederico videotaped the entire event, his camera glued to his eye. "After all," he said, "it's not every day my nephew gets accepted to a Hollywood film-making school. If that isn't cause for a party, I don't know what is!"

But Uncle Freddy was just acting happy and pleased. I could tell that it was an act. Behind the smiles and joking, my magician uncle was hiding something from me, but I didn't know what.

After cake, Uncle Frederico ordered all the dogs, cats, lizards, turtles, and birds that were family pets out on the front lawn, and I forgot my worries. Maybe I was imagining things.

"Atten-tion!" Uncle Frederico waved his one free hand while the other still clutched the video camera. "All animals in their proper places."

And the dogs, cats, lizards, turtles, and birds hopped, twitched, slid, and scrambled obediently into lines that spelled the words *Goodbye, Drac*.

Goodbye, Drac. Goodbye to me.

My name is Drac (Dragomir) Johnson, and I have a confession to make. I am a fourteen-year-old wimp warlock. Well, half warlock to be precise, and half red-blooded thoroughly human teenage boy. The fifty percent warlockian part comes from my mother's side of the family, the Mandoris, and the fifty percent "normal"

2

part comes from my thoroughly human father, John Ballard (J. B.) Johnson, golf nut and computer salesman.

Was I making a mistake? I worried. In another hour I'd be saying goodbye to all my crazy relatives and boarding the plane for Los Angeles International Airport. I'd be leaving the safe, if somewhat wacky, supernatural community of Eerie, Pennsylvania, a special section of Erie City, and heading toward a new school with normal—one hundred percent human—kids. Would I be able to fool them? To keep my half-boy/half-warlock status hidden?

Sensing my unspoken doubts, my beautiful dark-haired mother pulled me away from grinning Uncle Frederico and the swarm of barking, meowing, hissing, chirping Mandori pets.

"Drac, what is it? Are you having second thoughts about going to a new school?"

From under the cloudy mass of black hair that framed her face, underwater sea green eyes blazed out at me.

I was still a baby to my mother. I knew she didn't want me to go away, but I couldn't back down. The school that had accepted me was none other than the famous Hollywood Offspring of World-Renowned Legends Junior High School, better known as H.O.W.L. High. H.O.W.L. High was a private, one-of-a-kind school that specialized in the very things I most loved: the mechanics of creating and producing horror movies. It was well known for its training in special effects and stuntwork. I was a klutz in the spell department, but I knew my way around tumbling, vaults, and free-falls. And I was obsessed by monster movies. Talk about a dream come true. A school made for me.

"It's not too late to back out, Drac," my mother suggested softly.

I stared into her shining green eyes and was almost hypnotized into staying home. Then Aunt Idreen's pet tarantula, Tiffany, jumped from my aunt's third hand and slid down the neck of my T-shirt.

That decided me.

"I'm going. I'm getting out of here," I snapped as I wriggled and danced in an effort to shake Tiffany loose.

Goodbye, tarantulas, flying broomsticks, magic spells, and all that hocus-pocus stuff I could never learn. I was going off to live in a normal, totally rational human world.

"Time for Drac to go," Uncle Frederico loudly announced, pointing to his unusual sundial watch. He pulled me aside and said in a low voice, "Now, you call me from this school of yours at the first hint or shadow of trouble." He stopped short as if he'd bitten his tongue, then grinned down at me. "But there won't be any, right? No trouble at all."

My uncle was behaving as if he was as worried as my mom.

All my supernatural aunts and uncles, cousins and pets crowded around saying goodbye, offering advice.

"Is your suitcase all packed?"

"Did you bring a jacket?"

"Sure you don't want me to take you to the airport?"

Aunt Tagoor slyly winked and held up her broomstick. "No traffic jams on this baby, I guarantee."

"Er, no," I said hurriedly. "Dad's taking me. In the *car.*"

The adventure was about to start.

H.O.W.L. High, here I come!

2

Shock. Surprise. Horror.

I got out of the cab in front of H.O.W.L. High just in time for school—my plane was hours late—and did a double take. Lurching up the path to the front door to the school were monsters, including a black-caped Dracula, two phantoms of the opera, and a handful of mummies! I spotted even more monstrous sights then: furry and fanged werewolves, zombies, witches, ghouls, and grisly nightmare-shaped monsters, moaning and drooling, and all advancing straight toward me! What was going on? This was a "normal" junior high school with one hundred percent *human* kids? If this was "normal," I'd get right back on the plane and take Mandori magical madness any day.

"Hey, kid, you forgot your suitcase!" the cabdriver yelled. Before I could stop him, he hurled my bag out the door, grabbed the money from my hand, and took off, leaving my fate to the foul fiends rapidly advancing on me.

Advancing—and then sweeping right past me. In through the huge double doors of the school.

Something that looked like the Incredible Melting Man—either that or he was a walking pizza—raced by. As he passed by close to me, I saw his makeup and realized he was no more a monster than all the other monsters, vampires, and aliens screeching past. He was just a kid in makeup. They all were!

"Hey," I said. "What's going on?"

He stopped and looked at me with a blank expression.

"The costumes, Frankensteins, Slime People . . .?"

"Spirit Week. First couple of days at school we're allowed to go a little wild to get into the rah-rah spirit." Incredible Melting Man peered more closely at me. "Hey, man, what are you supposed to be? I can't place the costume."

Neither could I. I wore jeans and an old black T-shirt, topped off by my favorite jacket: jade green with the words *Kindred Spirits* in red and purple encircling a fire-breathing dragon and an eagle. My mom's talent-model agency was named Kindred Spirits, and she had created the jacket.

I thought quickly. What was I supposed to be? Make up something, *anything*.

"Uh, well, uh—Attack of the Humanoid Broccoli People."

"Wow, must have been some underground horror flick I missed. Broccoli People. Are you a stalker? Get it? A mad stalker. Broccoli People 'Stalk' by Night." And throwing back his head, Pizza Man screamed with high-pitched laughter before moving inside.

And I knew that I, ol' Humanoid Broccoli Stalk himself, had to get a move on and join the other kids. I couldn't stand outside all day, suitcase in hand, staring nervously at the entrance. It was some entrance, I had to admit, and deserved a second look. Actually, it was some school.

Although colorful exotic flowers and palm trees lined the driveway, the gates and stone facade of H.O.W.L. High looked like a medieval fortress. A fortress or castle out of a spooky old horror movie, with arched stained-glass windows and towers that boasted the strangest-looking gargoyles I'd ever seen. On a ledge peering down from the roof were large stone bats, their eyes crossed, which gave them a comic, rather than sinister, flavor. Stone vultures spread their wings, waiting, I could almost guess, for a student to stagger out of class and collapse. If we were going to make monster films at H.O.W.L. High, then the atmosphere was perfect. There was even a life-size statue of—could it be?—Edgar Allan Poe, standing guard on the front lawn. He looked remarkably silly with an open book in one hand, a mask in the other, and a stone raven perched on his shoulder.

As I stood there, the monster mass pushed and jostled past me. I took a deep breath, fingered the lucky red dice I always carried in my pocket, and walked into the school. What I noticed first was the noise. Metal lockers lining the walls banged loudly. Kids, dressed in their crazy costumes, screamed and laughed and called one another names. In the midst of all this racket a teacher was running back and forth yelling directions that everyone managed to ignore.

Wheee-eeet! He blew a whistle and then screamed, "Seventh graders go to Mrs. Kabargo's room."

Wheee-eeet! "Will all new students and eighth and ninth graders go immediately to the auditorium for the principal's talk."

My ears pricked up. New students? That was me. But what was I supposed to do about my suitcase or finding out about my room? In a few minutes the hall emptied out. Now it was just me and a few costumed stragglers. A cardtable had been set up right in the middle of the black- and white-checked floor. The checkerboard floor was polished and cold, and huge marble pillars ran from it up to a high arched ceiling. Sunlight streamed through the purple and green and red stained-glass windows and cast a glow over the entire hall.

Wheee-eeet! "You there! You're late, late, *late!* Where do you belong?"

The teacher put his hands on his hips and glared at me from beside the table. He was a tall, loose-jointed, nervous-looking man with tufted brown hair and a habit of constantly wetting his lips and blinking from under colorless lashes.

I walked over to him and put my suitcase down. Up close I could read his name tag: Mr. Hackerdorf. "Mr. Hackerdorf, I'm a new student. Ninth grade. I know I'm late, but my plane was delayed, see, I flew all the way from—"

"Name?" he interrupted. "What's your name, name,

9

name?" His lips were practically twitching from nervous tension.

"Uh, Johnson. Dragomir Johnson."

He bent down and his head bobbled over a clipboard on the table. "Johnson, Johnson, Johnson . . ." He slid a finger along a column of names and then looked up at me, his eyes blinking suspiciously. "You're not listed."

"Not listed! Wait a minute. I've *got* to be listed. I have a letter from your placement office and one from the principal to prove it. Look again, please?"

He stared at me in silence and then picked up his clipboard.

"Sorry. No Johnson, comma Dragomir. Only Johnson, comma Tony."

"But—"

"No Johnson, comma Dragomir. See for yourself."

At this point two of the stragglers sensed something was going on and drifted over to the table. One was dressed as Dracula, the other as a tree. Before I could figure out what horror classic had a tree for a lead, I had the clipboard thrust into my face.

I ran my eyes down the columns of "new students" and did a double take.

"Well, what the—!" I exclaimed. "It's right here. Just like I said."

I pointed an indignant finger at the *Johnson, Dragomir* that loomed boldly in black before *Johnson, Tony.* "What do you call that?"

Now Dracula, the tree, and Hackerdorf all leaned over to stare at the name. The teacher gasped. He stabbed his whistle at my name. "I call that Mandori, Dragomir.

Mandori, young man, not Johnson. Mandori, Mandori, *Mandori!"*

What! I checked again and blinked. Sure enough, the *Johnson* had rearranged itself into *Mandori.*

Mom, I whispered under my breath. I know this is your doing. Now please quit the tricks and let me be who I want to be at this school—a human Johnson and not a magical Mandori.

There was a moment in which I could feel my mother invisibly working her power right there in front of Hackerdorf. The air was charged with her energy, but I had power, too. I squeezed my eyes shut and concentrated on keeping my human name on the sheet.

"Well, I never!" exclaimed Hackerdorf, making my eyes pop open. "It *does* say Johnson, plain as anything. I never, I never, I *never!"*

The kid in the tree suit, stocky build, intense snapping eyes, nudged Dracula and then pushed past a babbling Hackerdorf to plant himself in front of me. (Which wasn't too hard to do in the costume he had on.) With one hand he picked up my suitcase and handed it over to the teacher, and with the other he began to propel me past the table. Dracula fell into step with us.

"Johnson, is it? Dragomir?"

"Drac."

"Drac, I like your style," the tree asserted. "There's something *different* about you. And in a school where 'different' is the norm, that's saying a lot. I'm Wiz, by the way. Winkleman Pruscott to be exact, but everyone calls me Wiz." He snapped his fingers and indicated his friend. "And this is the Count."

11

"Cornelius Spelvin." Dracula grinned, baring his teeth to reveal ridiculously overlong wax fangs. "Better known as the Count. I'm very Vlad to meet you."

He nearly clicked his heels as he took my hand and bowed over it. Cornelius, or the Count, was short, chubby, and blond. If there was anyone who looked less like the Prince of Darkness, it was this kid. Still, his Transylvanian accent was good, and he carried himself with style.

"Pleased to meet you, Count," I said. Both the Count and Wiz moved me right along, away from the whistle-blowing Mr. Hackerdorf, down a long wing that opened on to a beautiful lawn with emerald green grass and an Olympic-size swimming pool. H.O.W.L. High wasn't as medieval as I had first thought. Before I could admire the view, my two newfound friends swept me into a huge auditorium that resembled an old-fashioned movie theater. It was packed with kids: kids racing up and down aisles, kids talking in their seats, kids on the stage, wildly dancing to piped-in rock music. Several teachers stood up front and tried to restore order, but no one paid a bit of attention.

"Let's sit close to the stage," Wiz instructed the Count.

Like a linebacker, the chubby black-caped boy dodged and elbowed people aside so we could march to the very front of the auditorium and slip into empty seats. Once settled, I leaned back and glanced around me. The room was really something, mysterious and spooky, in keeping with the rest of H.O.W.L. High. Chandeliers out of a horror movie mansion glittered suspended from the ceiling. The stage had red velvet curtains, tied back with golden tassels. Above the stage was a painting of a hand, no, a claw, rising ominously out of a misty swamp. Written in the mist were the initials *S.E.* Before I could ask what it meant, Wiz nudged me.

"Get ready. Showtime."

"Showtime," echoed the Count in gleeful anticipation.

Offstage a gong sounded. Like a shot, the kids dancing on the stage stopped and raced down the steps to find seats. Someone switched off the music. All the screeching, laughing, and yelling faded, and an electric silence surged through the auditorium. The gong sounded again, and then a brawny, short man bristling with energy marched rapidly onstage. He looked like a pickup truck wedged into a business suit. When he reached the microphone to the right of the stage, he stopped with the precision of a soldier and squared his shoulders. As if on cue, kids sat up straighter in their seats.

"Who is this guy?" I whispered to Wiz.

"Big Dukes Madrix," said Wiz, his eyes never leaving the stage. "The principal."

The military-looking man stared intently into the quiet group of students as if willing them to pay attention before he began.

"Filmmaking," he said in what could only be described as a growl. "Filmmaking is what we're all here to learn. But let's not forget that H.O.W.L. High is a junior high school with regular courses in math, English, history, languages, and science. You came here to learn to make movies, but in order to make movies, you need to

13

have a solid, well-rounded education. Let me explain how our school can help you."

Clasping his hands behind his back, he proceeded to deliver a short but electrifying lecture. All around me kids were staring up at the stage, completely silent. When Big Dukes Madrix wound down his patriotic speech about the wonders and privileges of attending H.O.W.L. High, every last one of the kids sitting in the auditorium seemed to buy the message, including me. I couldn't wait to go to my very first class.

"Here comes the best part," the Count whispered, rolling his eyes. "Miss Popularity Princess herself, addressing her adoring fans."

Wiz snorted. "Admit it, Count, you're just mad because Lisa got an A in LeBaron's film history course last year and you got a—"

"Never mind what I got," the Count hurriedly cut in. "That isn't the reason she bugs me and you know it. She's bossy and a Miss Know-It-All."

Wiz nudged the Count as Big Dukes stopped speaking and glared straight at us. He waited for silence and then continued.

"And now, I know you'll welcome our Student Activities Commission president, Miss Lisa Horowitz, who will talk to you about H.O.W.L.'s involvement in the nationally sponsored Horror Junior Filmmakers Competition." He leaned over the podium and practically raked the crowd with his fierce eyes. "We're going out for this important award—and we're going to win it. HOWLettes, come on and do your stuff!"

The crowd began to roar even before the four cheerleaders in short skirts and letter sweaters raced out on to the stage. Could this be true? Could I be seeing what I thought I was seeing? Were there really four girls inside those Halloween-colored costumes, the short skirts of pumpkin orange, the sweaters of midnight black with tiny metallic skulls forming the school's name? I couldn't tell. Each girl wore a hideous werewolf mask. To make the spectacle even sillier, they threw back their heads and howled between chants.

"H-O-W-L,
And we're going to give 'em—L-W-O-H.
Bet you that we win first place.
Hypnotize 'em! Exorcise 'em! Poltergeist 'em! Yeah!
H.O.W.L. High!"

Each girl in succession jumped in the air and did a split, pom-poms held high. The crowd sent them off with their own howls and wild applause.

A girl dressed as the Catwoman walked up to the podium then.

"Knock 'em dead, Lisa!" Wiz yelled and grinned when the Count made a face.

She waited for the noise to stop and began to talk about the horror competition. I listened at first but tuned out to examine her more closely. So this innocent creature was the object of the Count's less-than-positive remarks. Lisa Horowitz sure didn't look mean or bossy. Right then, standing up on that stage in a black leotard and tights, she looked like a kitten, slender and delicate, with a small pointed face and pretty catlike features.

Her hair was midnight black, shiny and perfectly straight, with heavy bangs that drew attention to her eyes, which were light colored. I wasn't sure if they were blue, gray, or green, because they were almost hidden under a curtain of hair and thick lashes.

Just at the moment that she lifted her head, my lucky red dice turned themselves over in my pocket and gave a tiny clicking sound. Being special dice, a gift from my magician uncle, Frederico the Phenomenal, they were supposed to click whenever something was about to happen, but whether that something was good or bad, the dice couldn't tell. Of course, my being a klutz in all things magic meant that the dice worked only fifty percent of the time.

They did begin clicking wildly when Lisa Horowitz paused in her speech and stared at me for the very first time. Her clear whatever color eyes widened and met mine without blinking.

Click. Click. Click. The red dice told me something was going to happen!

3

I don't remember too much about the rest of the assembly except that Lisa Horowitz kept staring at me. And with the magic red dice clicking, she was giving me the creeps. Finally, after Mr. Madrix wrapped up the program and dismissed everyone, Lisa raced off the stage and up to our seats.

"You were terrific, as always," Wiz greeted her, unfolding his trunk and standing up.

The Count didn't say a word, only hissed and drew his cape over his face.

She ignored both of them and turned to me. "You've got to be in our project. You've just got to. I knew it the minute I laid eyes on you! You'd be perfect!"

"Project? What project?"

"For the horror film competition. You'd be perfect for our film, I can feel it." She wheeled around and faced a somewhat surprised Wiz. "Wouldn't he? Isn't he absolutely the *best?* Oh, who is he? Where did you find him?"

"He's a new kid, Drac Johnson. I swooped him away from the jaws of Hackerdorf."

Her eyes sparkled excitedly. Strange hazel-colored eyes with a ring of green around them. I'd never seen anything like them, not even in my mother's Mandori clan.

"Drac?" she cried. "As in Dracula? Oh, it's too perfect!"

"Dragomir," I corrected.

"Dragomir," she repeated thoughtfully. "What kind of name is that?"

Warlock, I should have said—if I wanted to be truthful. But I didn't. I wanted to hide my Mandori background from these kids.

"Uh, my father's from Tennessee and my mother's from—well, she named me for her grandfather." At least that part was true.

"I'm Lisa Horowitz, by the way. We have to become friends fairly quickly since we're going to be working together." And with that she smiled and leaned over to shake my hand. On her arms were ten or more silver bracelets, all in the shape of snakes. When she moved, as she did nonstop, she jingled and jangled.

"Whoa, back up!" I said. "I never said I'd be in your project."

Boy, she *was* pushy and more than determined. Maybe the Count wasn't off-base about this girl after all.

Lisa just smiled this of-course-you're-going-to-be-in-this-project kind of smile and shook her head. "Wiz,

Corny"—the Count actually winced when she called him that—"look at Drac. I mean, really look at him. Who does he look like?"

Both the Count and Wiz put their heads together and stared at me in silence. The Count stroked his chin in Draculian fashion and smiled an evil smile. "Blood Type A, all the way."

"Not what, you dope! Who! Be serious," Lisa snapped.

"Mighty Mouse? The Blob? Rambo?" Wiz threw up his hands. "I give up. Quit the suspense, you're killing me."

"Shadow Man. He looks exactly like Shadow Man." She began ticking off items on her fingers. "He's tall, with just the right sort of build, lean yet athletic without being Mr. Muscle Beach. He's got gorgeous black curly hair, a little long but we can always cut it, fantastic bone structure, and the eyes. Just look at those eyes! If they aren't Shadow Man's, I don't know whose are!"

"You're crazy," Wiz said.

The Count continued to peer intently at me. Now he was staring at my eyes as if they were chocolate-covered grasshoppers.

"We-e-ll," he murmured and coughed. "I hate to admit it, but maybe she's got a point, Wiz. Drac does have the same kind of eyebrows."

"Forget the eyebrows," Lisa said. "Look at his eyes! Did you ever see such a hypnotic color? Why, they're the most fantastic—" She paused, struggling for just the right adjective.

"Blue," said Wiz.

"Green," said the Count.

"Silver!" Lisa cried. "What are all you talking about! He's got silvery eyes, like moonlight on snow, like Shadow Man's."

"Well, actually," I said, "they're brown."

That was only one quarter true. My eyes *were* brown, but also green, or blue, or silver gray, depending on the angle of the person staring into them and the state of my emotions. Variety of eye color was a Mandorian blessing —or curse—depending on how you looked at it.

Right then it was definitely the latter.

I hurriedly pulled out sunglasses from my jacket pocket and put them on. They were a gift from Uncle Frederico on my thirteenth birthday, shiny mirror shades that prevented people from looking in but allowed me to look out. Uncle Frederico was my mother's eldest brother, and the sole "professional" of the Mandori family (Fabulous Frederico the Phenomenal— Magician Extraordinaire!), and the glasses he gave me had supernatural properties. They picked up and beamed messages and sometimes transmitted visions, views of steamy green jungles with birds of paradise or the tops of pyramids on vast stretches of Egyptian sand. It was rare that I glimpsed such sights, as my receiving powers were weak, but when I did, it was like stumbling into a dark movie theater, not knowing which film I was going to see. Was it going to be funny? Thrilling? Or scary?

". . . the Shadow Man movies, don't you?"

Lisa's voice startled me back into the wonderfully all-too-human world of H.O.W.L. High.

"I'm sorry. What did you say?"

"You're not going to get your way this time," the Count said with a smug grin. "Drac's not even listening to you. Not everyone's crazy about Shadow Man, you know."

At that my ears picked up. Shadow Man was my all-time favorite horror movie character. "Yes, I am."

It was Lisa's turn to smile. "Then you've seen the Shadow Man movies?"

"Who hasn't?" I said. "Next to Boris Karloff's monster and Bela Lugosi's Dracula, Rondo Orlac made the most terrifying fright flicks ever. I remember being scared out of my mind the first time I saw a Shadow Man movie on TV. I had nightmares for a week. That creepy two-headed emperor of the universe sending his secret weapon, Shadow Man, to suck up Earth people's intelligence. Ugh. I still get the creeps whenever I think about Shadow Man hissing and slithering in the dark, like some huge killer cobra."

"I liked the stunts best," Wiz said, "when Orlac was half man and half shadow. No other movie made in the fifties and sixties came close. I still can't figure out how he crawled up those buildings or leapt off cliffs."

"He was more athletic than Batman, that was for sure," the Count agreed.

"Spookier than the Wolf Man," said Wiz.

"He had—probably still has—the biggest cult following of any actor in a horror flick," I said. "Especially since he fell to his death while filming. What I can't understand is how someone as well trained as he was

21

could have leapt off that tower without using any safety measures. It's a mystery."

"Exactly," Lisa agreed enthusiastically. "That's why we're making our movie about Shadow Man. The movie that's going to beat out all the other competition in the contest. You know that after Rondo Orlac died, no other Shadow Man film has ever been produced. But we're going to finish that last movie of his as a tribute to him, and we're going to do it right on the actual sets Rondo Orlac used."

My mouth hung open. "But I thought the tower and surrounding sets were permanently shut down and locked. No one's been allowed to use that area in years."

Lisa tossed back her shiny black hair and laughed. "That's why it's so wonderful that we've been given permission to shoot our film there. A TV crew from 'Entertainment Now' is coming to the old Specter Empire movie studios, which happen to be right next door to H.O.W.L. High, to do a special on Shadow Man. They're going to be unlocking the tower and all the sets for the first time in twenty-five years! The ban has officially been lifted, and Specter belongs to H.O.W.L. Now don't you see how our project can't go wrong? We'll have all this fantastic free publicity. Our Shadow Man movie has to be a smash. But only if you agree to play him."

I was definitely interested. Me take on the role of Shadow Man, one of monster movies' most beloved yet feared stars? A man who made history when he mysteriously plunged to his death in his last, and supposedly most commercial, hit in the late 1960s? Lisa Horowitz might be a bossy, never-take-no-for-an-answer kind of person, but I decided to play the part of Shadow Man for my own sake.

The decision to accept must have shown on my face because Lisa let out a delighted whoop and Wiz cried, "Congratulations!" The Count pulled me aside and wiggled his eyebrows in Lisa's direction. "Are you sure about this? Working with us and our group means having to bow to the orders of the Popularity Princess."

"I want to do it," I said firmly. "I can deal with Lisa."

"That's what everyone says," the Count said. "But you'll see."

Before I could see anything, I had to get my suitcase and find out where my room was, so the four of us marched back to Mr. Hackerdorf.

Five minutes later my newfound friends and I were standing in the door of my assigned room—gazing in horror at the window.

The private rooms for boarders at H.O.W.L. High were in the school building—girls on the second floor and boys on the third. The floor was black linoleum, the walls monastery gray, and the cot, dresser, and desk toy size, but the sunshine streaming in through the multicolored glass of the small leaded window brightened up the room. It was all very cheery and reassuring until suddenly a dark shape from outside the window lunged against the glass!

And that's why we were standing frozen in horror, like one of the exhibits in Madame Tussaud's Wax Museum.

Tap! Tap—tap—tap.

23

The *thing,* giant claw, whatever it was, knocked sharply on the glass.

"Wha-what is it?" I asked and dropped my suitcase.

"I don't know." Goose bumps had broken out on Wiz's arms, tree bark and all.

Tap—tap—tap!

The dark blur remained just outside the stained glass, its knocking growing more menacing, more . . . ominous.

"Tell me this is a joke," I implored. "Some kind of stunt kids pull on new students?"

Lisa had gone pale. Her enormous hazel-colored eyes were fixed on the window. The girl who hadn't seemed afraid of anything was very frightened now. And that didn't reassure me one bit.

Tap—tap—tap!

"What should we do?" whispered the Count, sidling closer to Wiz. All of us moved closer to one another until we looked like a giant human octopus, with arms and legs shaking.

"Open the window," said Lisa between clenched teeth. "We've got to."

"What do we mean, *we?*" the Count croaked. "It's not my window! It's not my room. It's not my visitor."

"Maybe it'll go away," Wiz added. But even as we stood there, waiting, the thing grew more violent. It whirled like a demon outside the glass and then struck, again and again.

"Oh, for heaven's sake!" I cried and, whipping up my courage, raced to the window and cranked it open.

24

Behind me, Lisa whispered urgently, "Drac, be careful!"

I squeezed my eyes shut as I heard the stunned gasps behind me.

And then opened them as I felt the thing come bursting in the room.

No demon bat, or claw from hell, but a creature about a foot long, winged and feathered, gray with iridescent patches on its plumage, intelligent, beady little eyes. It swooped with ease over our heads.

"Gruesome Ghouls, what is it?" the Count cried, flinging his cape over his face.

Lisa uttered a little scream that trailed off into nervous giggles.

"It's a bird," she sputtered. "Just a bird."

But she was wrong. She was as wrong as she could be. It wasn't just a bird.

It was a pigeon. *My* pigeon, to be exact, and it had flown nearly three thousand miles to see me.

My witch mother had a cat for a familiar to do her bidding, Aunt Idreen had the tarantula Tiffany, Cousin Baal-ez his lizard Sam, and I had a pigeon named Hawk. When I had my "coming out" party, I botched up certain words in my "familiar" ceremony. The arrogant hawk that should have been mine to command—*poof!* —was turned into a pigeon.

Yet the nature and personality of a hawk remained inside that harmless, almost laughable body. Hawk had become a close pet and companion to me in the year since I got him, a part of the Eerie scene I hadn't wanted to leave behind when I was accepted at H.O.W.L. Yet sometimes he could still drive me crazy.

As he was doing now, by showing off in front of my friends, doing loop-the-loops, ruffling his plumage. I decided that no one could know he belonged to me, since that part of my life was a secret. I could see that he had a message for me— a tiny scroll was tied around his neck. I didn't know how I was going to get it.

"Of all the stupid, ridiculous—" I began, trying hard to treat Hawk's presence like a joke.

Wiz was hopping on one foot, rocking with laughter, his whole leafy body shaking, while the Count was baring his fangs and pointing a warning claw at the pigeon.

"Vait until my bat gets hold of you, my little delicacy," he intoned in his Dracula accent. Now that he was over his fright, he was laying on Transylvania pretty heavily. "You'll make a delicious pigeon pizza."

Lisa had stopped giggling and was following the whirling, playful flight of Hawk with interest. "What a beautiful coat he has," she said. "I've never seen such radiant colors on a pigeon before." She tilted her head and looked across at me. "I've also never seen a pigeon behave that way before. It's strange."

"That's Dragomir for you," Wiz said with a small smile. "He attracts strange behavior, even from birds. I knew it the minute I saw him pull one over on Hackerdorf."

Hawk landed on the dresser and stood there, preening his feathers for Lisa to admire. Before she could see the tiny message around his neck, I darted in front of her and fixed him with a glare that commanded, Don't move. He stood still, only bobbing that silly little head of his and ruffling his feathers. With a lunge I grabbed for the scroll and managed to get it off his neck.

But then Lisa cried, "What are you doing to that bird? Don't hurt it!" and I dropped the tube of paper.

"Look!" Wiz said. "The pigeon dropped something!"

"It-it's nothing!" I cried. "Just a rotten peanut!"

All four of us leaned down at the same time to reach for the mysterious object and bumped heads. In the confusion Hawk swooped down and picked up the scroll in his beak and waddled off. He flapped his wings and managed to avoid any of the outstretched hands that so eagerly grabbed for him. Hawk had been assigned the task of delivering a message to me. He knew the importance of getting the message into my hands—and my hands only.

We must have looked ridiculous—three kids and a warlock chasing a pigeon around a dorm room. Then the Count tripped on his own cape and fell forward, his hands out. He made contact with Hawk.

"I've got him!" the Count crowed.

But Hawk knew a few tricks. He wasn't a Mandori pet for nothing. He slipped out of the Count's stubby fingers and made for the window. For one second he perched there, turning his head to look straight into my eyes. And then he ducked his beak and took off.

We all rushed to the window, but I got there first and stared forlornly at Hawk's departing body. But then I looked down, and there it was! Hawk had dropped the scroll on the narrow window ledge. He hadn't failed in

27

his task after all. Floating back to us on the air came one savage screech, one that a hawk might have made.

"That is one crazy bird," Wiz muttered, standing beside me. "One crazy bird."

"Anything goes at this school," I said mildly. "I wouldn't call H.O.W.L. High exactly normal."

And while the three of them laughed about the pigeon adventure, I turned away and secretly opened the note. What would it be, a funny message from Uncle Frederico? A be-sure-to-take-your-vitamins-and-we-love-you note from my mom?

With a smile on my face I glanced down at the note—and the smile froze.

There were only four words, but they sent a sudden chill through my body.

Beware of your shadow.

It was a joke, sure, it must be. A silly joke from Uncle Frederico or one of my Mandori cousins. That's what I told myself and managed to smile as I crumpled the note and shoved it into my pocket.

But why were my hands shaking?

Why had the sun disappeared behind clouds and left the room bathed in a sinister greenish light?

It was a joke.

4

I didn't tell anyone about the note.

How could I? They'd think I was crazy, and Wiz already thought I was strange.

I could just hear their questions: "And exactly *how* did you receive this note?" "And you say this pigeon is really a pet named Hawk and flew three thousand miles to find you—" Pause, raised eyebrows. "How did this pigeon that's really a pet named Hawk know where your room was since we all just got there a few seconds before?" And last but not least, "What does the message mean?"

Good question. I was in the dark as much as anyone, most of all Lisa, the Count, and Wiz.

Beware of your shadow.

It didn't mean a thing to me. It had to be a stupid joke from the Mandori pranksters in my family. Sure, that had to be it, I told myself. A joke.

29

But later that night, after dinner in the old-fashioned dining hall and a lecture about the do's and don'ts of coed dorm life (mostly don'ts!), I found myself at the phone booth on my floor. I closed the glass door and stared at the graffiti on the wall: "Fangs for nothing!" "Godzilla's not fat, he's just short for his weight." "The Mummy will do anything in a bind." And on and on. Were these kids into movie monsters or what? Trying to manage a smile, I got my change ready and picked up the phone—to hear my mother asking nervously: "Are you all right?"

I hadn't even dialed! This phone trick she plays never fails to startle me.

"Mom," I said, "I'm fine. How did you know I was going to call?"

"I sensed something was wrong. I had my hand on the receiver to call you myself just now. So what is it, Dragomir? What's wrong?"

"Mom, I keep telling you, I'm fine. There's nothing wrong. I was just calling to—uh—tell you I arrived okay and the school's great. And, oh, I forgot," I added as casually as I could, "did anyone send a message to me? Uncle Frederico or one of the cousins?"

"You mean through Hawk? No. Why?"

My heart sank. I sat down abruptly on the small stool. "Oh, no reason. It's nothing important. Say, is Dad there?"

My father's warm, southern accent reassured me and also made me feel a little homesick. When my mother came back on the line, I was feeling better. She asked if I was having any trouble making friends with one hundred percent human kids, and I put her mind at rest.

"Hey, I've made three great friends already," I boasted. "They're making a creature feature for some horror competition, and they've asked me to play the lead!"

"Creature feature? You mean like a monster movie?" My mom sounded surprised—and a little uneasy. "You in a film? Who, or what, do they want you to play?"

"Just the creepiest monster in movie history," I began excitedly, but stopped short when the overhead fluorescent lights began to flicker on and off. Suddenly the long deserted hallway was filled with shadows. Deep, dark shadows that seemed to move as I stared at them.

"Drac," Mom said with a touch of impatience in her voice. "What are you going to play?"

I tore my eyes away from the deepest, darkest patch of blackness in the hall and felt my magic red dice click together. "The Shadow Man! I'm going to play the Shadow Man.

"It's fantastic. You ever hear of the Shadow—" I was cut off before I could get the name completely out. Metallic static, harsh and cold, jammed the line.

"Mom?" I said. "Mom, can you hear me?"

Through the blanket of noise I could barely make out her voice.

"What? What did you say?" She sounded tiny and millions of miles away, as if she were calling from Jupiter.

Instantly the line went dead. In the sudden silence I

could hear a funny sound, a muted sound of something slithering. It was coming from the end of the hallway next to the pocket of darkest shadow.

I took a deep breath and, still grasping the receiver, opened the phone booth door. Complete silence. Not a peep. Not a slither. I almost laughed with relief until I heard the sound again. My heart began pounding. The dice in my pocket tumbled together crazily like teeth chattering in fright. There was someone—some*thing*—waiting in the darkness of the hallway. Something unknown and creepy and—evil.

"Hello," I whispered. "Who's there?"

The rustling sound stopped. But the silence had a hollow, waiting feel to it.

"Who is it?"

Beware of your shadow. The words flashed in my mind. Beware of your shadow. *Shadow.* I felt the stirrings of unreasoning panic. Because it hit me that the slithery sounds in the hallway were exactly the slithery sounds Shadow Man made in his horror films when he was out stalking victims in the dead of night.

"Who's there?" This time I shouted.

I squinted down the hall and swore I saw a shadow move before the overhead lights sprang back on. I collapsed against the wall of the phone booth and then jumped violently when something tapped the glass.

"Hey, you've been on that phone long enough! I've got an important call to make." A face, definitely human, definitely kid, peered in at me.

It was a guy named Jack Bateman. He was on my floor, in a room two doors down from me. His real name was

Teddy, but everyone called him Jack, as in Jack the Ripper, because he had a thing for gruesome slasher movies. But at that moment I loved Teddy Bateman more than I ever loved anyone in my life. He was sane and rumpled and annoyed looking, and he broke the unearthly hold the shadows held over me in the hallway. And there was the sound of a dial tone now coming from the receiver.

"The phone? Oh, yeah, sorry." Almost giggling in relief, I stepped out of the booth. "It's all yours."

I was letting my imagination run away with me. First with the note, and now with those rustling sounds. One of my smart-mouth cousins could have sent Hawk with the message as a gag because I was going to H.O.W.L. High. And those strange noises could have been made by the wind through a crack in the open hall window. Or by Teddy Bateman playing a joke on me. That would be just his twisted sense of humor. Sure, that had to be it, I told myself as I headed down the hall. Everything explained away in a logical and rational manner. I walked into the boys' Bat room (someone had painted out the *h*) with a smile.

Friday afternoon a week and a half later, Lisa and I were walking out of the school library right before lunch, my arms filled with what felt like barbells.

"Are you sure I have enough books?" I asked Lisa sarcastically, barely able to see her over the pile I was carrying. "I mean, I could probably squeeze in another one or two."

Lisa actually seemed to consider the question in a

serious way. "Well, these are all the books about the career and art of Rondo Orlac that I could find in the research section of the library, but we could try to look up other books that might include brief references to him."

She was all set to do just that when I stopped her. "I was kidding, Lisa. Joking. Look at what you're forcing me to lug around as it is, a pile of books so high I can barely see over them. And do I have to read *all* of them?"

"If you want to know everything there is to know about the great actor you're going to be playing, you do. And the sooner, the better."

I continued to grumble under my breath. You couldn't argue with Lisa. She always had an answer. If you listened to Lisa Horowitz, she always had the *right* answer. President of the Student Activities Commission, assistant editor of the school newspaper, *Frightlines,* she knew (or *thought* she knew) everything and everyone that mattered at school.

Walking down the hall next to Lisa was like walking down the street next to a world-famous rock star. Kids stopped her constantly to say hi or ask questions about an activity at school. She really was a whirlwind, the most energetic girl I ever knew, and all the time those snake bracelets of hers jangled. Maybe she was kind of cute with that long black hair and those unusually colored eyes, but her personality—give it a C——had gobs of room for improvement. Definitely. Much too bossy for me.

As if reading my mind, she shot me a sly look from under those dark bangs of hers. "Why do you think we're going to win this film competition, Drac? Because of all the extra work we're putting into it."

"Correction—*I'm* putting into it."

"And the sooner you start doing it, the better. As in *right now.*"

This was going too far. "But it's lunchtime! And it's Friday. I'm loaded with homework, and you want me to ignore not only all my other subjects, but the rumblings in my stomach to concentrate on Shadow Man?"

"That's right."

"But—"

"Hey, Drac!" Around the corner wheeled the chubby Count. "How about joining me, Wiz, and some of the other guys for lunch? We're sitting out back by the teachers' parking lot."

"Great—" I began but was cut off by Lisa.

"He can't," she announced in that no-nonsense tone of hers. "He has work to do. And it's for *our* project."

"Didn't you read your horoscope for today, Lisa?" the Count asked. He closed his eyes and wrinkled his brow, as if contacting someone in the Great Unknown. "Let's see, it says, 'Definitely, but *definitely* leave all new students alone at lunch.'"

"Very funny," Lisa said and sniffed.

"And, Drac, yours said, 'Good day to say no to anyone named Lisa.'"

Both the Count and I broke up over that one when Nyerrah King, a friend of Lisa's and a member of our Shadow Man project, came hurtling into view and practically knocked us over in her excitement.

"Lisa, we're in trouble! Big trouble!" Nyerrah cried.

35

"Mrs. Kreighley just told me that Drac can't be in our video competition without writing a paper about a certain aspect of filmmaking. Like the ones we had to do over the summer. It's one of the requirements for the project, and the deadline's, like, right now!"

"What! A paper?" I asked. "I wasn't told anything about reports or papers when I got accepted at this school. The only extra things I brought are tapes of me doing gymnastics." Not be able to be Shadow Man? I had been so excited—and now I was devastated.

"Wait a minute," Lisa said, thinking hard. "Drac can bring a gymnastics tape of his to Mrs. Kreighley's room and see if she'll substitute the tape for a paper. She could give him credit for it—if she wants."

"But—"

"No *buts,*" the Count chimed in. "For once Lisa's got a point. Give me all those books and go get one of your gymnastics' tapes. Then meet us in Mrs. Kreighley's room as fast as you can. I'll get the rest of the kids in the project to meet us over there, too."

I didn't argue.

I dumped the heavy load into the Count's arms and took off. Within seconds I had raced up the three flights to my floor, burst into my room (scaring poor Hawk, who was perched on my windowsill), and grabbed a tape lying on my closet floor. Then it was turn around and zoom back down to Mrs. Kreighley—and hope and pray she liked what she saw on my tape.

Coretta Kreighley was a tall, chunky woman in her fifties, with a fake-looking auburn-colored wig, a deep brisk voice, and false eyelashes so thick and furry they had to obscure part of her vision. But she was respected in the school, both as the vice principal as well as a teacher. Tough but fair, that was Coretta Kreighley's reputation.

Now I hoped she'd be kind. She had listened seriously to Lisa's impassioned plea to accept my tape in place of a report.

"We'll see" was all she said.

I handed over the tape and watched her pop it into the VCR. Lisa motioned for me to sit down and promptly found an adjoining seat.

"I hope she likes it," she whispered and held up crossed fingers. "I hope *all* the kids like it."

I turned around and looked at them, the Fang Gang: Lisa, Wiz, the Count, Nyerrah, a gloomy boy named Arnold, and a towering silent giraffe of a kid nicknamed Fist. They were sitting bolt upright in a circle around the VCR, anxiously waiting to see my video. Wiz caught my eye and smiled. I nervously smiled back. Please let Mrs. Kreighley like my work. Please let me be Shadow Man. The red dice in my pocket seemed to hiccup, making me jerk. Oh, no. What was coming next?

Too late to worry. Mrs. Kreighley inserted the tape, punched the Play button, and the video began. The *wrong* video! This was no demonstration of my gymnastic skills, but the home movie of my infamous going-away party, the one that my uncle had packed into my suitcase at the last minute. I reached forward to push the Stop button, but Mrs. Kreighley stopped me first. "No false modesty now—I have to see this tape."

There was absolute stillness in the room as the video continued and the audience was treated to an aerial shot of Aunt Tagoor's bridge club members practicing their dives and rolls on their broomsticks. I shuddered when the camera proudly lingered on the banner floating behind Aunt Tagoor's broomstick. It was a white silk sheet with the words *Dragomir's Going-Away Party!* That was Uncle Frederico's cute idea for the opening credits to the home video.

Six shocked faces—no, seven, counting Mrs. Kreighley's—stared goggle-eyed at the screen. I slouched deeper in my seat and closed my eyes. No need to watch. I knew all too well what was coming next, and there was no way to stop it.

Inside Mrs. Kreighley's classroom no one moved, no one blinked, no one whispered a word. All mouths hung silently open. Minutes passed, humiliating, drawn-out minutes, as the home video continued. Every now and then I'd half open one eye and glimpse things like my mother walking in with the huge farewell cake—without touching it; Cousin Wa'albi directing a cone of rain to fall directly and solely on my head; the Mandori uncles tap-dancing on the walls and ceiling. . . . And finally Uncle Frederico directing all the pets present to get into formation and spell out the words, *Goodbye, Drac.* But did he leave it at that? Oh, no, not Frederico the Phenomenal. He had the animals and birds somersault once in the air and then immediately get back into line.

The tape was over. My life was over. The embarrassing spectacle of the Mandori family had been revealed for all to see. My warlock connection had been exposed. The kids now realized I was a freak. I'd be ordered out of the project and dismissed from school.

Like Rip Van Winkle awakening, Mrs. Kreighley blinked a few times and made funny gestures with her hands. She was obviously trying to say something but struggling to find the right words. All around me the room slowly stirred into life. Wiz started shaking his head and couldn't seem to stop. Then he sat up straight and snapped his fingers.

"Fa-an-tas-tic!" he pronounced. "The best special effects I've ever seen!"

"Drac, you're a genius!" Lisa exclaimed, but she had a funny expression on her face. "Why didn't you tell us you could make movies like that?"

"And those talented character actors!" the Count said. "Can we see it again?"

"Yeah, let's see it again!" Arnold cried.

"Yeah!"

"You—*liked* it? I mean, you're not kidding me?" I couldn't believe my ears. My terrible secret had been exposed, but no one believed what they saw was real! My wimp warlock status was still safe and secret.

"Liked it?" Mrs. Kreighley laughed. "I think the verdict is unanimous. We loved it. You've certainly got a fine career in front of you in the horror genre, what with being able to combine humor and those special effects so cleverly. I'd like to talk to you sometime about how you managed to do those special effects . . . what trick photography you used and camera angles."

"So he's in?" Lisa asked. "Drac is in the project?"

"He's in," everyone chorused. "He's our Shadow Man!"

I could feel a huge grin split my face. And then I remembered the words on the message: *Beware of your shadow. Beware . . .*

Almost angrily I fished the scrunched-up piece of paper out of my pocket. I had been carrying it around all week. It was time to put the note where it belonged, in the garbage.

But when I opened it up, I got the shock of my life.

There was no message about Beware of your shadow written on the paper.

There was nothing on the paper at all. It was completely blank!

5

Something was wrong.

I could feel it the moment I was inside the main gate and looking up at the tower. The cold stone tower on the Specter Empire movie backlot where Rondo Orlac ended his Shadow Man movie career twenty-five years earlier. I sensed something that no one else on our special tour seemed the least bit aware of—a distinct chill in the air. Only the members of the Fang Gang and the small crew from the TV show "Entertainment Now" were listening to Principal Big Dukes Madrix welcome them to the historic opening of the locked Shadow Man building.

Big Dukes performed the honors because H.O.W.L. High now owned Specter Empire and because it was located behind H.O.W.L. High, which had originally served as the administration building for the horror movie company. Now I understood the engraved picture of the claw rising out of the mist above the stage in the school auditorium. That grisly little image was the logo for Specter Empire.

And speaking of things grisly, my eyes kept returning to the very top of the stone tower. Although it was a mild, sunny Saturday, an army of refrigerated ants tap-danced their way up and down my spine, making me shiver. The day before, in Coretta Kreighley's class, I had officially been chosen to play the part of Shadow Man. I should have been feeling proud and excited, but instead I felt increasingly nervous, as if something bad was about to happen.

And happen right in that tower where Rondo Orlac died.

I tried to concentrate on the principal's speech to stop thinking about those icicle ants.

"And we're here today," Big Dukes was growling, "to pay tribute to that fine actor Rondo Orlac, who lost his life so tragically while filming *Revenge of Shadow Man* in 1966. As you may or may not know, that incident occurred on this very set, from that tower behind us."

The principal swung around to point at the tower. All eyes followed. Someone in the "Entertainment Now" crew scribbled notes furiously while the host of the show, curly-haired giant John Dowling, whispered something to his assistant director. The sun had been hidden behind a cloud but now burst forth with eye-blinding brilliance. Without thinking, I pulled out my magic sunglasses and popped them on.

And sucked in my breath when I stared up at the top of the tower.

Outlined against the sky stood Shadow Man! Or, I hurriedly amended, someone in the purple and black hooded cape and costume of the movie monster. I couldn't see his face clearly, but he seemed to be staring down at us.

Down at me, actually.

He had his hands bunched into fists at his sides. Suddenly he extended his arms so that he looked like a bat—a bat about to swoop.

I took a step back.

That guy, that Shadow Man look-alike nut up there, was going to jump from the tower!

"Hey!" I shouted. "There's someone up there! He's going to jump!"

There was absolute silence after I interrupted the principal's rambling speech. Then commotion and confusion reigned.

"What's he talking about?" I heard John Dowling say.

"Is the kid crazy?" another "Entertainment Now" crew member asked.

Wiz hurried over and nudged me in the ribs, none too gently. "You're going to get us kicked off the set if you don't stop playing games. So quit it!"

I couldn't look at anyone. My eyes were glued to the top of the tower and that strange figure with its arms outstretched and its body poised for flight. It took a step closer to the edge. Another. One more step and—

"Someone get up there and stop him!" I yelled.

Big Dukes Madrix shouldered his way through the crowd and planted himself in front of me, his fierce eyes level with mine. When he spoke, his voice was ominously low.

"What do you think you're doing, Johnson?"

I reluctantly tore my eyes away from the figure on the tower and stared into the principal's angry face.

"Can't you see for yourself?" I asked, wondering why everyone was behaving so strangely. "You've got to get up on that tower and stop that guy from leaping off the edge."

"What guy? And kindly remove those sunglasses while I'm talking to you, young man."

I pulled off my glasses and pointed up at the tower.

"Why, that . . ." my voice trailed off in shocked disbelief.

No one was on top of the tower.

The Shadow Man impersonator had disappeared into thin air.

Impossible, and yet I knew that I had seen him. Had seen him clearly through my sunglasses. The *magic* sunglasses. Then it hit me. I had seen something all right, but it wasn't real. It was a vision beamed through the magic lenses. But, of course, I was the only one lucky (or unfortunate) enough to see it. And that's why everyone clustered around me wore such weird expressions on their faces. They looked at me as if they thought I was cracking up, maybe. Or had some serious emotional or mental problem.

"Yes, Johnson, I'm waiting," Dukes Madrix growled. "And your explanation better be good."

I realized I had some fast backpedaling to do if I wanted to hang on to my role as Shadow Man. Wiz, the Count, Arnold, and Fist all wore disgusted frowns, while Nyerrah was simply shaking her head back and forth. Only Lisa was looking at me with any degree of understanding. I didn't know why because she was usually the first one to fly off the handle at any real or imagined slight. It just felt good to know she was on my side, however stupid that side seemed to be.

The principal crossed his arms and narrowed his eyes. I had to think of something and fast. Thoughts flew through my mind, excuses, explanations. None seemed to work. "Well, uh, sorry, I—"

"Drac is our Shadow Man, so it's natural he should see the ghost, isn't it?" Lisa's clear voice cut across my stammered apologies. "I mean, there *is* a legend that the ghost of Rondo Orlac haunts the tower and only appears to an actor who tries to replace him as Shadow Man. Isn't that right, Drac?"

She was a lifesaver! Talk about brilliant excuses!

"Wait a second, that's a great idea to put in our show!" John Dowling explained. He snapped his fingers, and the scriptwriter hurried to his side. "Let's include this kid. What's your name, Dragomir Johnson? It'll be perfect for the intro to the show. Something like: 'Does the ghost of Rondo Orlac—no, change that to Shadow Man. Does the ghost of Shadow Man still stalk Specter Empire? A young actor playing him for a filmmaking competition might know the answer.' Blah, blah, blah, we can question this Dragomir and his friends about the school project and Rondo Orlac."

The assistant director began babbling with the script-writer while a very pleased John Dowling clapped Big Dukes Madrix on the back, assuring him that H.O.W.L. High could only benefit from all the publicity it would get on national television.

The principal's stern features actually relaxed, as did the faces of the Fang Gang. Huge grins replaced frowns. Wiz and the Count gave each other high-fives, while Fist picked up an unsuspecting Nyerrah and twirled her around.

"We're going to be famous!" crowed a normally gloomy Arnold, who then performed a sloppy cartwheel.

"All right, all right, settle down, people, settle down." Big Dukes held up a warning hand. "You're not movie stars yet, remember." He sounded as gruff as ever, but there seemed to be a twinkle in his eyes.

I felt a tap on my shoulder. Lisa was standing there, beaming at me.

"Oh, Drac, I *knew* you'd bring us good luck the moment I saw you, and I was right!"

She was so excited I thought she'd hug me, but just then the security guard arrived with the keys to the Shadow Man sets. Time for the big unveiling! The camera crew of "Entertainment Now" bustled around setting up their lights and equipment to record the historic event. John Dowling got his hair combed by a stylist and looked through his notes. Big Dukes cleared his throat and marched over to the double-locked doors of the building. I could sense another speech coming on.

While the assistant director called for a rehearsal and the "Entertainment Now" crew scurried about, the Fang

Gang lined up to watch what was happening with wide eyes. Everyone was too busy to notice when I slipped away to wander over to the tower.

I circled round the back of the gray stone building until I was out of sight. Some instinct, some feeling, drew me there. Was there really any truth in Lisa's improvised ghost story? Had the spirit of Rondo Orlac appeared to me because I was going to play the role of Shadow Man, a role the actor jealously considered his own? I had heard rumors of the director assigning Rondo Orlac's understudy to finish *Revenge of Shadow Man,* but something had happened to the understudy. Nothing so drastic as death, but some minor accident that convinced him to quit and not perform the tower stunt. As a matter of fact, there had been other attempts at Shadow Man movies that had all failed for one reason or another.

Unless the real reason had been standing on top of the tower, staring down at me only a few minutes before.

And had waited for me in the shadows of the deserted hallway at school last week.

And had sent me a warning note through my pet pigeon the very first day I arrived at H.O.W.L. High.

Beware of your shadow.

It all began to add up.

The icicle ants kicked into high gear again, scurrying up and down my spine. As if on cue, the sun slid behind a cloud. A cold little wind seemed to circle around me and lead me to the padlocked tower entrance.

Nervously I stretched out a hand to touch the lock.

Great, I thought in relief when nothing spooky happened. The way into the tower was blocked to me. There wasn't anything supernatural going on. I stood there for a moment, listening. No peep from the dice in my pocket. All silent. All clear. I could rejoin the others now.

Before I removed my hand, however, the padlock quivered beneath my fingers and slid open. The tower door creaked an inch or two inward. Had the wind done that? I thought.

What wind?

And no wind had jimmied the padlock.

I angrily rattled the dice in my pocket. Thanks for nothing, guys, I muttered. What a lousy time to go to sleep on me! As I slipped my hand out, however, they hiccuped into life, clicking like a baby Geiger counter.

I stood facing the wooden door. What should I do? All my human instincts told me to run. My Mandori instincts urged me to stand and confront my demons—or in this case, my ghost. I stood there, torn.

The door swayed a little, as if inviting me in.

The dice tumbled crazily in my pocket.

I put out a hand to slam the door shut when I heard a voice calling to me from inside the tower!

"All right, Johnson, you hightail it in here and meet me at the top in two seconds flat. I found something up here you'll want to see."

I'd know those gravel tones anywhere. It was Big Dukes Madrix. Somehow the principal had gotten inside the tower, probably through some other entrance, and now wanted to show me something. I couldn't understand it, but I recognized the principal's voice—and I recognized a command when I heard one.

"Yes, sir!" I called back. I pushed the door open and stepped inside.

And immediately fought back a feeling of panic when the door slammed shut. It was cold and damp and black inside. As black as the bottom of a lake at midnight. I took a few steps forward and bumped my knee against something.

"Mr. Madrix, sir, I can't see a thing down here!" I yelled with a quaver.

There was silence, then the reassuring if somewhat annoyed growl of the principal echoed down to me. "There's a light switch by the door."

I mumbled under my breath, but obediently searched the moist, cobwebbed stone walls until I located the light switch and flicked it on. A sickly yellow glow flooded the blackness from lightbulbs strung overhead. It wasn't the strongest lighting in the world, but it did its job in chasing away imaginary goblins. I could see now what I had stumbled against—a circular stone stairway. The stairway that led to the top of the tower and to whatever awaited me. I shivered in the murky yellow light.

But it was silly to be scared when Big Dukes Madrix was up there. No spirit. No ghost. And certainly no Shadow Man. A real live flesh and blood man. But then I thought, how did the principal manage to reach the top of the tower before me? Did he run all the way? Or was there something weird going on? I hesitated.

"Let's go, Johnson! On the double!" Dukes Madrix called in an irritated voice. He sounded human to me.

I took a deep breath and started to climb. There were at least eight stories to the building, judging from the arched windows at different levels. I wanted to look out but couldn't. The windows were boarded over. Around and around I climbed, not daring to look down. The light was murky, but I could still see how far I'd fall if I tripped.

At one point, midway up, I stopped to catch my breath. Was that really my heart banging away? It didn't help to know that the magic red dice in my pocket were twitching so crazily they felt like popcorn kernels about to explode. I cursed the Mandori strain that made me half-warlock and sensitive to supernatural atmospheres. I sighed and started to climb again when I heard a sound. Had that been the door to the roof? As if in response, a chilly gust of wind pressed against me like a fist.

"Mr. Madrix?" I called. "Are you up there?"

The gust of cold air that had swept over me was damp, and chilly, and somehow menacing, as if it came from a ghostly region. That was silly, of course. It was just cold air.

Or was it?

The wind turned into an Arctic mass that had somehow gathered evil force, and now it held me captive.

I couldn't move. I twisted and turned helplessly in the grip of the ice-cold wind.

"Mr. Madrix? Help me!"

The lights overhead grew brighter, then abruptly wavered and went out. The entire stairway was plunged in blackness. I was a prisoner in a stone tower, held against my will by an evil current of air and absolute darkness. My heart began racing in my chest, and then I heard the most wonderful reassuring sound.

"I'll help you, Johnson, just hold on." It was the principal's voice, but it sounded different somehow, deeper, slower, as if a battery were running down.

I was beginning to imagine the sound of bats squeaking overhead when I heard footsteps slowly walking down the stairs. Then I saw the welcoming glow of candlelight. The principal was coming to my rescue after all.

I began to breathe a sigh of relief until I saw who, or what, descended the stairs and came into view.

Shadow Man. A hooded and caped Shadow Man bearing a candle whose flickering glow made a monstrous mask out of half-hidden features.

The closer this thing came, the harder I tried to move. To run. To scream. But my lips were rigid and my knees were shaking and the icy fist of the wind kept me paralyzed.

When the figure was ten steps from me, it stopped. It lowered the candle, pursed its lips together, and began to whistle.

The hair at the back of my neck quivered to attention. The thing was whistling the theme from the Shadow Man movies.

"Do you know who I am?" The voice was deep and harsh, yet kind of ragged, as if it came from an old radio with poor reception.

51

The figure brought the candle closer to its face with hands that looked like claws. In the flickering light the face seemed to be all eyes—huge, black, and hungry.

I shrank back. The ghost of Rondo Orlac had spoken those words. I had seen too many of his movies not to recognize his distinctive voice or those large, gleaming eyes.

"You—you're—" I struggled but couldn't get his name out.

"Shadow Man," the figure said. "The one and only. And that's how I intend to keep it, Dragomir Johnson. Oh, don't look so surprised. I know all about you. The same way I knew all about the others who dared think they could play me on the screen." He lowered his voice to a dramatic hiss. "No one will *ever* play Shadow Man except for me. I *am* Shadow Man. And this is my warning to you. Listen well, or I will summon forth my shadow to seek you out and make you understand."

"But—"

Too late. The ghost brought the candle to its lips and blew it out.

At that moment the overhead lights went back on and the downstairs door crashed open. The ghost had vanished. And with it, the restraining force of the wind. Half running, half stumbling, pushing aside cobwebs, I flew down the dimly lit stairs and pushed out into the warm, welcoming sunshine. I took a few calming breaths before slamming the tower door. The padlock immediately relocked itself. Then it was a mad dash back to the "Entertainment Now" rehearsal at the entrance to the

Shadow Man building. The crew was taking a break, and John Dowling raised a hand in greeting to me.

"So there's our missing star! We'd been wondering what happened to you. Been seeing any more visions of Rondo Orlac lately?"

He was teasing. I deliberately kept my voice light.

"Oh, sure, without a shadow of a doubt!" But it was no joke.

The ghost of Shadow Man had warned me.

6

I spent all Saturday night sitting and thinking. And my thoughts focused on one thing—the little tower visit from Rondo Orlac. Playing Shadow Man in our school filmmaking competition could definitely be dangerous to my health. The ghost made that all too clear. But I didn't want to give up the part. Lisa was counting on me, as were the rest of my Fang Gang friends. And even if I turned down the role, they'd go ahead and select someone else. And then that poor kid would go through what I'd been going through, only he wouldn't have any warlock skills and talents to help him.

Besides, John Dowling and his scriptwriter were coming to Specter Empire the next afternoon to interview the security staff and other people connected with the history of the Shadow Man buildings and property. I had my own interview scheduled at one-thirty, and as vain as it sounded, I wanted to be on "Entertainment Now." I wanted all my family members to see me on TV.

The question was—would I live long enough for that to happen?

"I will summon forth my shadow to seek you out," Rondo Orlac had warned, "and make you understand."

I didn't know what that meant, but it didn't exactly sound like an invitation to a party.

Rondo Orlac meant business, which meant I had to take action before he made the first move. I had just made up my mind to go down the hall to call Uncle Frederico when I heard a sound at my door. I stopped midway across the room, my heart pounding.

"Who is it?" I inched closer to the door.

The scratchy noise continued, as if long, pointed claws were sharpening themselves on the wood.

"Who's there?" My voice rose. Indecisively I put a hand on the doorknob. Did I hear a rustling sound? Like a purple and black satin cape sliding across a polished linoleum floor?

I couldn't take it anymore. After yanking the door open, I immediately went into a karate stance and confronted an angry Hawk, who had been scratching away in an effort to get my attention. As soon as the door opened, he waddled inside and hopped up on his favorite perch—the window ledge.

I followed him inside with a scowl on my face. "Don't ever get locked out again!"

Hawk fixed me with a beady glare and shrugged his very much ruffled feathers. "Hmmmph," he seemed to be saying.

"All right, all right, I'm sorry," I apologized. "It's just this Shadow Man business is getting on my nerves. I'll make it up to you, I promise. I'll treat you to your favorite gourmet peanuts."

Hawk gave a satisfied squeak that signified all was well between us and we were friends. With that one problem taken care of, I now had to address another, far bigger one.

After grabbing some change off my dresser, I hurried out into the hall but came to a screeching halt fifty feet from the phone booth. Kids had been yelling and creating noise in the halls, but as soon as I put in an appearance, they all scattered, disappearing into their dorm rooms.

Had I done that? *Or something else?*

Was it a coincidence I was marching all alone to the phone, or the doings of a certain ghost? Now that I had seen Rondo Orlac up close, I knew he meant business. He would do *anything* to prevent me from playing Shadow Man. Would he go so far as to attack me in my own school?

I stood in the hallway, hands jammed in my jeans pockets, tense and unmoving. I kept remembering the way those midnight black eyes had devoured my face, the ugly threat in that wavery underwater voice.

"I'm not afraid," I said in a whisper. I stared up and down the hallway and addressed the deepest, darkest shadow behind the phone booth. "Do you hear me? I'm not afraid."

Somewhere in the mass of shadows, did something wait for me? Something invisible and coiled up as tightly as a rattlesnake, waiting to sink ice-cold fangs into my skin if I came too close?

I remembered who, and what, I was. I was a Mandori warlock. I took a deep breath and started to move.

"I am not afraid," I whispered, my eyes never leaving the nest of shadows. "Not afraid."

I came to within a foot or so of the telephone booth, mumbling under my breath the entire way. Then something touched my shoulder.

I screamed and jumped a foot. Behind me stood Wiz, a big grin on his face.

"You always talk to yourself, Dragomir?"

I made a face at him as he passed me, and I immediately felt better. Was Shadow Man trying to scare me, or was I doing it myself? I really needed to talk to Uncle Freddy. Luckily, my uncle was home and all too anxious to talk to me when I reached him. In fact, he seemed to know what I was going to say before I opened my mouth.

"You mean you know all about Rondo Orlac and his haunting of the Specter Empire tower and sets?"

"Why do you think I've been so nervous since you left for H.O.W.L. High almost two weeks ago?" Uncle Frederico asked. "I knew you'd be close to Specter Empire, but I kept hoping that you wouldn't bump into the ghost. And then your mom told me about your playing Shadow Man, and I knew it was only a matter of time before Rondo Orlac sought you out."

I was more than a little confused. I knew Uncle Frederico was a walking encyclopedia of all subjects ghostly or mysterious, so he'd know about the Shadow Man legend, but there was something else going on, something he was keeping from me. And when I asked, he didn't deny it.

"I hoped I wouldn't have to get into it, Drac, but, yes, Rondo Orlac and I met many years ago, when we were both just starting our careers. I was a beginning stage magician in Hollywood, and he was a young actor signed to do his first Shadow Man movie. We met at a dinner party. I had been hired to entertain the guests, all movie actors and directors. And Orlac took me aside at the intermission and asked me all sorts of questions about my magical abilities. I was young and vain and foolish, so when he accused me of being nothing more than a phony playing parlor tricks, I showed him *The Book of Shadows*. That's one of the Mandori books of spells and ceremonies handed down from generation to generation."

My uncle paused, then gave an angry snort and continued. "Do you know that not more than an hour later, when I was doing the second half of the show, *The Book of Shadows* was stolen? To this day I believe that Orlac was responsible, although he denied everything at the time, and nothing could be proved."

I thought furiously. "If that's true, then he may have used spells from the book to help him with his more difficult stunts!"

"And that may be why he still possesses power even as a ghost," my uncle agreed. "And it drives me crazy to think my magic created such a vengeful spirit."

"Couldn't you have used your own powers to get the book back?" I asked.

"I tried, but Orlac outsmarted me by using a spell

58

from the book to prevent me from ever being able to get close to him. But as a Mandori, Drac, and now the next Shadow Man, you may be the one to get *The Book of Shadows* back. And I've got a plan that just might stop Rondo Orlac from haunting you or anyone else ever again. But you're going to have to have courage to do it."

Oh, great, I thought. A battle of the powers between a klutz fourteen-year-old warlock and an ageless jealous ghost. Somehow the odds didn't stack up in my favor, but if I didn't take action and do something, there wouldn't be any odds at all. Shadow Man would win, and the Fang Gang would lose. I couldn't let that happen without a fight.

"All right, Uncle Freddy," I said. "Let's hear the plan."

Sunday afternoon. Rain clouds massed overhead. If I didn't know better, I'd have said that Rondo Orlac had specially ordered them for the sole purpose of scaring me.

That day I would have to face the ghost as part of my uncle's plan. It didn't help to have the atmosphere as gloomy and forbidding as in an old-fashioned horror movie. I stood in the school lobby a little after one o'clock, peering nervously out a stained-glass window. Lost in my thoughts and worrying about the plan, I didn't hear or sense a thing until I felt a tap on my shoulder.

I whirled around and screamed. A ten-foot-high costumed Shadow Man swayed ominously in front of me! And then it collapsed as the huge cape opened to reveal

Lisa as she jumped down from the shoulders of Wiz, and the Count popped out from behind them.

"Go, Shadow Man!" the three cheered in unison, totally oblivious to the shock I was experiencing.

"Good luck at your interview!" Wiz offered with a grin.

"Mention my name," the Count ordered.

"Uh, yeah, real cute, guys," I managed to get out, but I was still shaking.

The blood must have drained from my face, because a concerned Lisa hurried up to me. "Drac, whatever's the matter? You look like you've seen a ghost or something."

Was she psychic, or what? "Don't be silly, nothing's wrong," I snapped.

"We didn't mean to scare you, honest." Her pointed little face stared intently at mine. For some reason she seemed to be reading exactly what was on my mind. But that was crazy, of course. Lisa Horowitz was no more telepathic than a telephone book. Yet I had to admit that since she saw the video of my Mandori going-away party, she had been acting different around me. She constantly peered at me in class or else sneaked peeks at me at lunchtime or during rehearsal for our Shadow Man movie. She was studying me for some reason, and I couldn't figure it out. It made me nervous because it made me feel exposed. Yet it also felt kind of nice to experience the connection with her, even if that connection was a mystery.

"Really," I insisted and managed a convincing smile. "I'm fine. And raring to go for the interview."

With shouts of encouragement still ringing in my ears, I left the school grounds and headed over to Specter Empire. Big Dukes had personally given me a permission slip earlier that morning, as well as a little lecture on what to mention (and what to omit) about the school.

"Remember," the principal had growled at me, "you're going to be representing H.O.W.L. High. Represent it well. We're counting on you. All right, that's all."

"Yes, sir!" I jumped to my feet and marched out of his office like a soldier on a mission.

Well, I thought, approaching Specter Empire, I *was* on a mission.

A ghost-hunting one.

The big guard on duty examined my note and waved me through the main gate. I hurried past movie sets and deserted phony city blocks until I spotted the Shadow Man tower. Even from that distance it caught my eye and commanded my attention. The "Entertainment Now" truck was parked beside John Dowling's awesome red Porsche. I stopped to admire the car before locating the giant-size host. He and the scriptwriter, a sour-faced man named Ed Purcell, were sipping coffee and discussing their notes in front of the Shadow Man building. Several other people were wandering about and nervously examining the sky. It did look like rain at any minute.

I squared my shoulders and approached John Dowling.

Phase one of the plan. Wish me luck, Uncle Freddy! I whispered.

"Excuse me," I said, "I'm reporting for my one-thirty appointment."

The scriptwriter made a point of examining his watch and raising an eyebrow. "Well, you're early. It's not even ten past. Besides, John's running late. There are two other people scheduled before you."

Just what I wanted to hear! But I needed to create the opposite impression. Seeing my crestfallen face—was I overdoing it?—John Dowling smiled sympathetically. "Look, Shadow Man, I'm sorry, but Ed's right. We are backed up. But hang around, and I'll get to you as soon as possible."

Here it comes, I thought, masking my excitement. Go easy, Drac my man, go easy. "Oh, sure, Mr. Dowling. Listen, do you think I could wait inside the building and just, you know, look around? I didn't get a chance to see it yesterday."

The "Entertainment Now" host hesitated. I crossed my fingers.

"Oh, sure, no one's in there except for the crew, but if you promise not to disturb them, why not?"

"Thanks—thanks, a lot!"

Trying to hide my eagerness, I slowly sauntered over to the large building housing the Shadow Man sets. Once at the door I stopped, almost sure John Dowling would change his mind and order me to return, but no one said a word.

I had no time to think about my interview. When the time came, I'd improvise, but right then I had far more important things to worry about.

Like phase two of the plan.

Like finding a menacing shadow behind me.

I took a deep breath and stepped inside the almost tomblike coolness of the building. Tomblike? Poor choice of words, Johnson. It was a cavernous space, as big as an airplane hangar, filled with rows of complicated (and probably dusty) cameras, arc lights, and props. To my immediate right the "Entertainment Now" crew was busy setting up equipment. Too busy to notice one terrified but determined wimp warlock—I hoped.

Trying to blend in to the background, I tiptoed past the crew and left the main hall, straight into a maze of corridors. Which way to go? I didn't have much time to snoop.

Hurriedly I pulled out the magic sunglasses and put them on, but they didn't help. The lenses only darkened an already dimly lit space and offered no clues or revealing visions. Scratch the glasses, I murmured, putting them back. That left the dice. If I remembered correctly, the dice had one function other than alerting me to danger—they could also *lead* me to danger. As much as I hated taking this emergency measure, I felt like I had no choice. Now if only I could remember how the Mandori spell went. . . .

I pulled out the red dice, placing one in my right hand, the other in my left. Closing my eyes, forcing myself to concentrate, I said aloud,

"Dice in my right hand,
Dice in my left hand,
Lead me to Orlac,
This I command!"

I brought the two objects together with a resounding bang, then waited. No puff of smoke appeared, no clap of thunder sounded, yet the dice rattled noisily, as if saying yes.

Score one for Dragomir Johnson. I grinned. I hadn't lost all my warlock ability. I held my hand open, palm up, and turned left. The dice were still. Oops, wrong way. I turned to the right, and the dice quivered into life and began clicking. Who needed a road map with directional dice to lead me? More and more quickly I moved, listening to the hiccups, burps, and clacking noises. Finally I turned down one corridor, and the dice nearly jumped a foot out of my hand. Even without the dice I would have known where I was. The air around me was charged with electricity.

I cautiously moved forward, head swiveling at all times in case the ghost would materialize. I passed door after door, realizing I had discovered the dressing rooms of the actors and actresses who had costarred or been featured in the Shadow Man movies. Down at the end of the hallway the dice in my trembling hand gave one last convulsive jump before lying still. I stood before a door with a huge gold star and the initials *R.O.* done in Gothic script. No guesses whose room this was.

Would the door be locked?

Would the door be open—with the ghost of Rondo Orlac waiting inside to pounce on me?

I stood in the corridor, hearing my ragged breathing and the faint sounds of the "Entertainment Now" crew from far away.

Time for the third and final phase of the plan.

I reached out, but the lock silently clicked on its own.

The knob turned.

The door swung open.

7

Swallowing nervously, I stepped inside Rondo Orlac's dressing room. All was quiet and dark. Maybe *too* quiet? Apart from the sound of my heart pounding, all was perfectly still.

Yet the ghost must be lurking close by, I reasoned. The lock didn't open by itself.

On that reassuring note I hurriedly pulled out the pocket flashlight I had brought along with me in case of emergency and turned it on. It wouldn't be too smart to turn on the lights for a security guard to notice and investigate. The weak little beam of the flashlight would have to do. I gently shut the door behind me and played the light around the room. The movie star certainly knew how to pamper himself. His dressing room was as big as four H.O.W.L. High dorm rooms together, and a heck of a lot nicer. I guess you could almost call it a suite, with Oriental rugs on the floor, expensive-looking paint-ings on the walls, and swanky leather sofas and chairs besides a dressing table and antique mirror.

There were also plenty of cobwebs hanging from the ceiling and a thick layer of dust sprinkled over every-thing. I guessed when Rondo Orlac died, the producers had temporarily shut and locked the door until a new Shadow Man could be chosen. But Rondo Orlac had made certain no other actor got to play his role or take over his dressing room, so the suite was like a tomb. Ugh, *tomb*—there was that word again.

I made a face and forced myself to get back to the business of searching the dressing room. Uncle Frederico had told me on the phone the day before that if Rondo Orlac was still able to use his powers, he must be using the stolen *Book of Shadows.* And because the actor had died so unexpectedly, the book was probably where he had left it so many years ago—close to his Specter Empire dressing room. It stood to reason because no mention was ever made of this extraordinary find when the personal effects in the actor's mansion were cata-loged.

"That means," Uncle Freddy had said, "my *Book of Shadows* must have been hidden by Rondo Orlac in his dressing room when he was filming *Revenge of Shadow Man.* And if you can get into it, nephew, you have a good chance of locating the book."

And once I had the book, time for a whole new game plan.

But first things first. I'd worry about that later.

As silently as possible I began to search. I pulled up

sofa cushions, peered under rugs, looked behind paintings. Nothing to be found. Then I started on a filing cabinet in the corner. The whole time I played detective, I felt as if invisible eyes were watching my every move. It gave me the creeps, but I didn't stop what I was doing. Drawer after drawer, file after file, I continued skimming old movie scripts, fan letters, studio memos—but no *Book of Shadows.*

I shut the last drawer with a mounting sense of frustration. Come on, come on, I muttered. Where are you hiding? I swung the flashlight around. Suddenly the beam caught and reflected in the large rectangular mirror. The glare blinded me for a second. I shut my eyes tight, then opened them again.

The flashlight gave a little shiver in my hand and died.

The room was plunged into darkness.

High above me rain drummed on the roof, and then a crack of thunder split the silence.

Great, I thought, terrific. I'm playing in my very own horror movie, and I get to be victim. There was no use clenching my hands in a maniac grip on the flashlight. They went right on shaking.

It was dark in the room, but there was another darkness that at that moment seemed to be moving toward me. Coming close, closer, almost close enough to touch. The room seemed to hold its breath, and then a light glowed in the antique mirror. A shape stirred in the depths of the glass. Something formed, the image of a face. As if coming from light-years away, it seemed to take forever to reach the surface of the glass.

Finally confronting me in wavering lines was Rondo

Orlac. Once again he was dressed as Shadow Man, and the hood on his head gave his features a sinister cast. I didn't want to look at him, but something about the light in his eyes caught and held my attention. The actor's eyes were dark and cold, but every once in a while a light would flash out of them. It reminded me of lightning across a stormy sky.

Rondo Orlac pointed a clawlike finger at me to move closer.

I took a step back. I wished I were watching him on a TV screen in the safety of my house back in Eerie. But this was no TV.

This was a mirror only five feet away, and the piercing, silver-colored eyes seized on mine with an intensity I found frightening.

"So we meet again," Rondo Orlac announced with a snarl deep in his throat. "And so soon. It's so nice of you to pay me a social visit. Or perhaps the visit isn't social at all? Perhaps you're here for some other reason?"

His lips twisted into an ugly smile that scared me more than any frown.

I tried to speak, but I couldn't get any words out. All I could do was shake my head from side to side, as if denying his unvoiced question.

Rondo Orlac threw back his head and laughed. The sound was cold and razor-sharp.

"I know your little secret, Dragomir," he said. "I know the only thing on your mind is finding *this!*"

Without warning the ghost whipped something out from behind his back and held it in front of me.

My heart stopped. The small black object danced in

front of my astonished eyes. The gold letters in the title winked at me. *The Book of Shadows!*

"Here," taunted Rondo Orlac. "Want a closer look?"

To my shock he thrust the book through the glass surface of the mirror, so that it waggled only a few feet from me.

Without stopping to think I jumped forward and snatched the book from his hand.

The actor was as startled, as completely taken aback, as I was. His mouth dropped open. His skeleton fingers scrabbled helplessly in the air, but his arm only seemed to be able to reach a foot from the confining prison of the glass.

He let out a howl of fury. "How could you take that which is mine? I own *The Book of Shadows,* yet it jumped from my grasp into your hands!"

I flipped open the front page, understanding dawning. There in elaborate script was the Mandori name, with the ancient date of the book's origin.

Now it was my turn to smile. I held the page open before Rondo Orlac and pointed to the name.

"There, you see?" I announced proudly. "Mandori. The book belongs to its rightful owner."

Bewilderment warred with fury on the ghost's face. "But you are *not* the owner. You are a Johnson— Dragomir Johnson!"

I drew myself up. "I am also a Mandori, from my mother's side. And this book belonged to my uncle, Frederico Mandori, before you stole it from him."

"Him? Bah!" The ghost spat. "That weak excuse for a magician!"

"That weak excuse for a magician helped you become a star through this book," I snapped. "And now I'll be able to use the book myself to remove the curse you've placed on Specter Empire as well as the Shadow Man character."

The actor pressed himself right against the glass and pointed a threatening finger at me. "You will never, *ever* play Shadow Man! Is that understood? You may have temporary custody of the book, but you will never be able to use it. What you don't understand, you adolescent fool, is that I still have a power to command and fulfill my wishes. And I command my power to do this—"

With a snap of his fingers a length of red silk cord appeared in his hand. The cord slithered in the air like a charmed snake and then jumped across the space to twine itself around *The Book of Shadows!* My fingers tried to undo the knot, but it would not loosen. If anything the cord drew more tightly together. I stared down at the book in horror. The way to stop Rondo Orlac from haunting me was as hidden to me now as it had been before I got the book.

I tried to think. I couldn't be beaten this easily, I just couldn't. Perhaps Uncle Frederico would be able to make some sense out of Orlac's latest victory.

As if reading my mind, the ghost in the mirror laughed.

"Have fun fooling around with the knot while you can, young Mandori. I promise *The Book of Shadows* will be back in my hands very soon, and there's nothing you or your uncle can do about it. And one last prediction: You will *never* play Shadow Man. I am Shadow Man, and Specter Empire is my home. You will never get me to leave."

And with a ghoulish smile the face of the horror movie star began to fade. As the image faded, the light dwindled in the glass. I stood there in silence as the room darkened, both hands clutching my book.

When the ghost had completely disappeared, the flashlight came back on. Reassured by its weak but comforting beam, I found my way out of the room and shut the door. There was a click as the lock turned on its own.

I stared down at the doorknob but saw Rondo Orlac's face there instead.

"Someday you won't haunt this building anymore," I whispered. "You'll be released, and I'll play Shadow Man."

Slipping the book in my pocket, I hurried back to John Dowling and the "Entertainment Now" crew.

"Drac! Hey, wait, where are you going?" Lisa cried. "We want to hear all about your interview!"

"How many times did you mention my name?" the Count asked. "I hope it was at least twenty—otherwise, I'll sic my bat on you!"

The members of the Fang Gang were waiting for me in the school lobby when I returned at two-thirty, but I hurried past them.

"John Dowling talked to me, but they had to postpone the shoot because of the rain. I'll tell you all about it as soon as I dry off," I said.

I was soaked to the skin by the downpour and anxious to get *The Book of Shadows* hidden somewhere safe. I ran upstairs to my room and spent five minutes trying to find the perfect spot. Hawk was underfoot the entire time. Bypassing my sock drawer, mattress, or desk, I finally placed the book inside the zip compartment of my suitcase. I locked the suitcase and stowed it way in the back of my closet. Someone would have to be Houdini to get to this book.

Rondo Orlac could open locks.

I felt a sense of panic until I realized he was probably able to perform that little trick only in the actual Specter Empire buildings. I really didn't believe he could materialize as Shadow Man at H.O.W.L. High. But then again H.O.W.L. High had been part of Specter. No, I decided, as long as I stayed put, the ghost couldn't get me.

Or could he?

"Think positively, for pete's sake," I commanded myself. "Don't let Rondo Orlac frighten you." I gave myself a little pep talk while Hawk listened from his perch on the windowsill, head bobbing up and down in what I hoped was agreement.

I really hadn't done too badly that day, all things considered. I had used my wits against the ghost and taken possession of my uncle's book. Now I'd have to sharpen those wits if I wanted to beat Rondo Orlac at his own game and get that red silk knot untied.

Only one person could help me with that.

I hurried down the hall to the phone booth and waited while someone finished a conversation. While I waited, I glanced up and down the walls, along the floor, in half-opened doorways, anywhere a shadow could be lurking. Even as I told myself I was safe, I heard a rustling noise. It came from the blackness at the very top of the window directly above the phone booth.

I didn't want to look up. I was afraid I'd see reptile yellow eyes staring down at me or a twisted mass of ugly shadows, wriggling together like snakes in a basket, sliding, sliding, sliding down the wall in my direction. And once the hissing shadow got to me? Would it leap onto my body and start draining me, just as the Shadow Man did to his victims in the movies?

I tapped on the glass of the phone booth and made impatient faces. The kid inside gave me a weird look but got off the phone. I dashed inside and slammed the door. Safe. (For the time being.) I called Uncle Frederico, who picked up on the first ring.

"Drac, I've been waiting to hear from you!" he cried. "How did it go?"

"There's good news and bad news, Uncle Freddy," I began, then told him everything that had happened to me in the dressing room. At the end of my recital, my uncle let out a worried whistle.

"I don't like the sound of this," He said. "Ghosts aren't supposed to be able to command red strings to tie into knots, or lock or unlock doors."

"Don't forget the electricity failing and the flashlight dying," I added gloomily. "Or what looks like a shadow moving and whispering in the hall."

"Shadow?" Uncle Freddy's voice sharpened. "You didn't mention that before!"

"I didn't want to say anything, because you know

74

Mom. She would have gotten all upset and nervous and demanded I come home."

"Well, I'm glad you said something about it now. That shadow reminds me of a spell from the book Orlac stole from our family. Now, if only I could remember it. . . ."

"While you're busy thinking, Uncle Freddy, I'll be working hard at getting the knot untied. I get the feeling I don't have much time. And speaking of Orlac, uh, you don't think I'll be paid a nighttime visit by Shadow Man, do you?"

"Of course not!" Uncle Frederico declared in so certain a tone that I breathed a sigh of relief. "However, I'd keep my doors locked and Hawk ready to attack just in case."

"Very funny," I said. "Very funny."

Only I wasn't laughing as I returned to my room and promptly shut and locked the door.

I turned to Hawk. "Know any good dive-bombing techniques?"

8

Earth to Dragomir Johnson! Earth to Dragomir Johnson! Come in, Dragomir Johnson."

I felt a ball of wadded-up paper hit my face before I looked across at a grinning Wiz.

"Ah, our Shadow Man isn't a space cadet after all," he announced.

"I wouldn't be too sure of that," the Count piped up. "It only took a full minute to get his attention."

He and Wiz laughed, but Lisa was staring at me with a strange blend of annoyance and concern on her face. "It's not funny," she said. "Drac isn't paying attention to rehearsal, and you other guys keep fooling around. You may think it's a joke, but the deadline for our film is less than two weeks away."

It was Thursday, September twenty-second, four days after my session with Rondo Orlac in the mirror. The

Fang Gang was meeting at lunchtime on the front lawn of school to go over the script. We were sprawled on the grass at the base of the large Poe statue, enjoying the sunshine and mild temperatures. Well, Wiz, the Count, and Fist were enjoying the sunshine, goofing around, while Lisa, Nyerrah, and Arnold sat up straight and worked hard on their lines.

I, on the other hand, did neither. Behind the pages of my script I kept working at the red cord that locked *The Book of Shadows*. Try as I might, I could not open the cover an eighth of an inch. For three days now I had picked at the red cord, sliced at it with a razor, tried to cut it in two with the sharpest scissors I could find. And with what results? The back and front covers were still stuck together like a cement sandwich.

It wouldn't take magic to undo the red silk knot, I glumly decided, but a miracle. Our completed project had to be cut, edited, and postmarked no later than Monday, October third. That gave us about ten days in which to finish rehearsing and then film. So far nothing disturbing had happened, but I half expected Rondo Orlac to show up at any moment. No way would the jealous ghost allow me to step into the role of Shadow Man. That's why I had to concentrate on the knot. The answer to stopping Rondo Orlac before he stopped me was in *The Book of Shadows*.

"Dragomir Johnson, have you heard a word I've said?" Lisa's irritated voice cut into my thoughts. I shoved the book inside my script and flipped it closed.

"I'm sorry?"

77

Nyerrah and Lisa exchanged pained glances. Lisa tapped the script.

"Your cue, Drac. I've said my line three times already!"

"Oh, right, my line, wait a sec—" I opened my script and fumbled with the pages when two things happened at once: The shadow cast from the Edgar Allan Poe statue slid a few inches closer to Nyerrah, and the Shadow Man dialogue on my sheet blurred and went out of focus. Too out of focus for me to make out, let alone read.

Something squirmed just beyond the corner of my eye. I looked over at Nyerrah, where I thought I saw the movement, but everything was perfectly still.

Too still?

Had the shadow on the ground changed shape? Had it slithered closer to Nyerrah? Was it just a basic, normal sunny day shadow—or something else?

Across from me an impatient Lisa waved the script in front of my face. "We're waiting for your line, Drac."

"Oh, yeah, just a minute while I find it. . . ."

I bent over the page again, but then I saw that funny little movement again. This time when I glanced up the shadow had definitely slipped closer to Nyerrah's legs. The black shape had grown larger. It resembled a hooklike hand, ready to pounce. Even as I stared at the shadow, it made a small hissing noise. Danger, it seemed to whisper. Danger.

My heart began pounding. "Nyerrah," I began in a warning voice. Before I could finish the sentence, the black mass pounced on to Nyerrah's legs, and she jumped up with a scream.

"I felt something!" she cried. "Something . . . I don't know, all chilly and damp."

Fist made a face. "Big deal. Maybe you were sitting in spilled soda or water. So move to another spot."

Nyerrah reached down to pat the grass. "It's perfectly dry and warm. I don't get it."

"We're not going to get it, either, if we don't stop all this fooling around and focus on the script," Lisa ordered.

Nyerrah gave Lisa a hurt look before she plunked down a few feet beside me. "I wasn't fooling around."

"All right, sorry," Lisa apologized. "Can we just get back to work and Shadow Man's first line? Drac?"

I squinted hard at my dialogue but still couldn't make it out.

"I can't read it."

"Oh, for heaven's sake, what's next?" Lisa cried. "I typed that myself, and the lines are perfectly clear. Let me see it."

Before I could move, Fist screwed up his face and gave out a yelp. He jumped to his feet and rubbed at his pants. "There *is* something cold and clammy out here! It's gross!"

"I told you," Nyerrah said. "I wasn't making it up."

"What a bunch of babies," Wiz snorted. "Getting all bent out of shape over a chill in the air or a wet spot in the grass."

There was no chill in the air or any little wet spot. This

was a message sent by Rondo Orlac. A message sent to warn me. Even as I stared in horror at the inky black mass only two feet from Wiz, I sensed the presence of ghostly evil. There was evil in the shadow, in the rustling of the trees, in the sudden damp breeze. There was evil all around me, and it was threatening the Fang Gang.

A sound as loud as a car alarm went off in the Mandori part of my body. Rondo Orlac was right there on the front lawn of H.O.W.L. High, and he was giving me a warning: *Stay away from the Shadow Man role, or I'll hurt your friends. Just see if I don't.*

I watched in alarm as the shadow gave another threatening hiss and leapt across at Wiz.

"Hey!" he cried out in shock and rubbed at his hand. "Something just sprayed me with ice water! And it hurts!"

"Feel your hand," Fist ordered. "I bet it isn't wet."

"Oh, for pete's sake," the Count said, shaking his head. "I can't believe you guys. What is this, some practical joke?"

"Are you calling me a liar?" Wiz demanded. For once his good-natured smile was strained.

"How about what I felt?" Fist added. "You think I made that up?"

My friends began raising their voices and arguing with one another as a result of being touched by the shadow. As if gaining force by the anger and fear among the Fang Gang, the dark black mass began to swell. Now the hooklike hand with grasping fingers turned in the direction of Lisa, who was so wrapped up in yelling at Wiz she never noticed a thing.

How could she not *see* the ugly twisted shape worming its way to her side? How could she not *hear* the cold hungry sounds it made as it got closer and closer? That awful hissing noise that reminded me of rattlesnakes preparing to strike, the same sound that Shadow Man made in his films? Couldn't Lisa see and hear the danger? Couldn't Wiz or Nyerrah or any of my friends? Obviously not, because if they could, they'd be leaping to their feet and racing as far from the evil shadow as possible.

How could I get them to go? In a matter of seconds the squirming mass would be all over Lisa, and now that it had gotten larger, I dreaded to think what it could do to her. To any of the Fang Gang, if they remained on the lawn in its path. I might not be able to send the shadow away, but I could get my friends to safety.

I got up as casually as I could, hiding the book in my jacket pocket, and then placed two fingers in my mouth and whistled. It was loud and piercing, and all arguments stopped. Everyone turned to look at me.

"I just remembered," I improvised. "Mr. Mendoza wants to see me in the gym to rehearse my fall from the tower. You know how concerned Big Dukes and Mrs. Kreighley are about my stunt. I've promised to go over and over it with Mr. Mendoza to make sure there's no chance that I can get hurt."

It wasn't really a lie. I did have a session with our school's stunt coach, but it wasn't scheduled until after school.

Lisa looked surprised and a little put out. "Well, I

guess you've got to do it, then. But what about our rehearsal?"

Out of the corner of my eye I saw the dark shape spill a little bit closer to Lisa's foot; it raised itself up, preparing to strike. In a second or two it might envelop her completely.

I ran over to her and picked her up to move her out of danger. She squealed and screamed, but I didn't care.

"The Shadow Man says same time tomorrow, how's that?" I asked, depositing her quite a good distance from that menacing threat.

Things didn't look good, I reflected as I watched my friends get up, grumbling and squabbling with one another.

Rondo Orlac was *not* giving up. I may have taken *The Book of Shadows,* but he still had the power to track me down and do some damage. I had saved my friends from him that day, but what would the evil ghost do next?

I made it through Thursday night by locking my door and sticking a heavy bureau in front of it. A shadow could slip under cracks, I reasoned, so I put drops of water around the floor of my bed. Mandori magic said that ghosts couldn't cross a body of water. Truth or fiction? I'd never had to test the theory before, but I wasn't taking any chances after seeing and hearing how powerful Rondo Orlac was. I even placed Hawk on active duty: He was to stay awake all night and guard the door.

Friday night after dinner I had just returned to my room when I remembered something. I had left my jacket in the dining room—and *The Book of Shadows* was in the pocket! Garbling some excuse, I dashed down the hallway and bumped smack into Lisa, who had my jacket in one hand and *The Book of Shadows* in the other.

I stopped dead. Act natural, I cautioned myself. Nice and natural and calm, as if nothing's wrong.

"You left these things behind," Lisa explained. "I was just coming to find you."

Natural, Drac, old buddy, nice and natural. I got my breathing under control and reached for the jacket.

"Hey, thanks. I really appreciate it."

Lisa handed over the jacket but held on to the little black book.

"What is this, Drac? And why is it all tied up in a knot?"

"Oh, uh, just a little gift from my family," I explained. "I keep it bound like that because—because . . ."

Nothing came to mind. I drew a total blank.

"Because you can't get it open?" she suggested. She tossed her bangs out of her eyes and gave me a funny look.

"Here, let me give it a shot. I'm good with knots, you know."

"No!" It came out a shout. I quickly lowered my voice. "I mean, thanks for asking, but really, no problem."

Once again I reached for the book, and once again she eluded me. Giving that little irritating laugh of hers that said I-can-do-anything-just-wait-and-see, Lisa began pulling at the red cord. Ridiculous to think she could make any sort of headway while a Mandori warlock couldn't, and yet the knot actually seemed to move in her hands. Her fingers made strange motions. The red cord resisted, fought against her, yet finally loosened with an angry pop.

"Hey, this string must be really old!" Lisa exclaimed. "But look, Drac, I got part of the knot undone."

I stared at her in shock. Impossible. Incredible. Unbelievable. Yet the knot was beginning to unravel. There was no time to waste.

Grabbing the book, muttering thanks, I took off for my room, leaving a bewildered Lisa behind. I needed to see if I could finish the job Lisa had started. But before I got there, the Count came puffing up the stairs.

"Drac! You've been invited to the TV lounge for a surprise!"

"I can't. I'm, uh, working on something."

The Count grinned. "You'll drop everything when you find out what the surprise is. Nyerrah got a gift from her parents that she wants to share with the Fang Gang. It's a videotape of the greatest moments in the Shadow Man movies, and it even has footage of scenes from the last movie Rondo Orlac made, and never finished, *Revenge of Shadow Man.* Don't you want to see it?"

I stood there, thinking, covering the book with my jacket.

"Come on, Drac. We've been given permission to watch the tape tonight, and even Mrs. Kitler from the kitchen is getting into the act by making us popcorn. How can you pass that up?"

I was all set to do just that, pass on the offer, when

something clicked in my brain, a little mental nudge from the Mandori side of the family. I'd learned early on to obey those funny nudges; otherwise, I'd regret it later. Not knowing what to expect, but deciding to obey my impulse, I turned and followed the Count down the stairs.

Something was going to happen, I thought.

Something to do with Shadow Man.

I didn't know what it would be, but I was ready to find out.

9

An hour later I still didn't know why my Mandori side had prompted me to go to the TV lounge. I sat on the battered sofa with my friends squeezed in around me, staring at the video of Shadow Man clips, but learning nothing new. My fingers were itching to work on the cord around the book instead. I squirmed nervously, and my magic sunglasses fell out of my shirt pocket and landed on Lisa's lap. She picked them up and twirled them around.

"Hey, careful with those!" I exclaimed. "They're mag— I mean, they *matter* to me."

"Big-time movie star glasses," she said with a grin and shoved them on my nose. "Here, big-time movie star, let's see how you look."

I blinked at the suddden darkness and started to pull them off.

Until I glanced at the screen and froze.

Rondo Orlac's mansion, a creaky old house on the outskirts of Hollywood, was on the tube. Apparently, this house was now a museum filled with props and costumes from the Shadow Man movies. The narrator, one of Rondo Orlac's fellow actors, was taking the viewer on a tour of the museum and had just entered the basement of the mansion.

"Now, this is where Rondo Orlac liked to come to relax," the man was explaining, "with private screenings of his films."

The camera panned a large room that resembled a fancy movie theater. It had several rows of seats, a large projection screen at least five feet high, and a circular space outlined with Greek columns and statues just behind the seats. The host plopped himself down in one of those seats and talked about his own visits to the special theater, but I saw something different. Through the lenses of my magic glasses I saw ghostly outlines of Rondo Orlac when he was alive and living in his house! The actor was standing in the space with the funny columns and marble statues. He was holding the Shadow Man mask in one hand, *The Book of Shadows* in the other! As he put the mask on, I saw he was wearing the Shadow Man ring as well. There was a large purple candle and a few other things on the floor around him. He flipped open the book and held it high. Then he began to read.

Even as I sat in the cozy TV lounge with my friends, I began to feel a chill. It crept in and swirled around my feet, my neck, my hands. But this icy little breeze did not come from the ghost of Orlac. What I saw on the screen through the powers of the magic sunglasses made me shiver and my teeth chatter all on their own. Rondo Orlac was performing a spell. He was calling forth a shadow from out of the spooky candlelit darkness. From that point on, I blocked out everything around me to focus on his words, the things he did. If I remembered them all, could I get control of his power? Could I stop the ghost from haunting Specter Empire, haunting me and the Fang Gang?

I leaned forward, straining to hear. The actor's words were faint, as if coming from another planet, but I could just make them out: "Shadow of Orlac, I command thee, come to your master and obey me."

When Rondo Orlac uttered that phrase three times, the fat candle burned down nearly to the end. A huge black shape on the projection screen made a jerky move, like a bat flapping its wings, and suddenly sprang into the air to land in front of Rondo Orlac. I blinked in shock. The shadow Orlac had called forth was the same one that had scared all my friends the day before! I didn't need my Mandori abilities to know that. The ghost of Rondo Orlac could command this evil shadow to do whatever he ordered. Well, now I knew the spell to summon his shadow, too. Maybe if I could call forth the shadow, I could command it to untie the knot. It would be a step in the right direction.

Staring at the TV screen, beginning to feel a sense of hope that I could end the nightmare, and do it all on my own, I suddenly realized that I wouldn't have a chance unless I had the Shadow Man mask and ring that Orlac used. Hope started to crumble. How could I get my hands on them? They were part of the Shadow Man estate and would probably be kept locked up somewhere. But where? I squeezed my eyes shut and thought.

"The museum!" I cried aloud. "That's where they are!"

Everyone jumped a foot at my outburst.

"What's he talking about?" Wiz demanded, frowning at all the popcorn he had spilled on his lap.

"That's where *what* are?" Lisa said.

I blinked at the screen, but Rondo Orlac had disappeared. The vision was gone. The show was over. Feeling embarrassed, I yanked the sunglasses off and struggled to come up with an explanation for my outburst.

"All the stuff having to do with Shadow Man," I said. "The costumes, and props and everything Rondo Orlac used when he was making the movies. They're at the museum, and, well—"

"I think we should go there," Lisa finished the sentence for me, almost as if she were reading my mind. "Drac's right. If we want to do a really great job with our film, we need to visit the Shadow Man museum. Maybe we'll find something, or learn something, we need for our project."

There was an excited burst of agreement from all the kids.

"But how can we arrange it?" Arnold looked at us with his usual gloomy expression. "We can't just hop on a magic carpet and fly there. It's over in Hollywood."

"We can ask my parents to take us," Nyerrah said, jumping to her feet in her excitement. "They're visiting me tomorrow, driving up from San Diego in the van, and I know I can get my dad to go to the museum. He loves all that old movie stuff, and horror stuff especially. He's more excited about the Shadow Man film we're making than I am!"

"But can we get permission from Mr. Madrix?" Arnold asked.

Lisa tossed her bangs out of her eyes. "I don't see why not. It's a Saturday, and he's always after us to, quote, broaden our minds, unquote. What better way to broaden our minds than to visit a museum?"

Almost by magic it was all arranged. I couldn't believe it. The Mandori "nudge" had helped me come a giant step closer to learning about the ghost of Rondo Orlac. The ghost I could handle, I thought.

But that awful black shadow?

Hawk squeaked indignantly as I prepared to leave my room early Saturday morning.

"You're not coming with us to the Shadow Man museum, so stop all that squawking. We don't need a pigeon playing Ghostbuster and that's final."

My bird ruffled his feathers and glared at me but finally settled down. Feeling guilty, I left out some peanuts for him and then closed and locked the door. Someone had to stay behind to guard *The Book of Shadows.*

Nyerrah's parents were waiting for us in the lobby, friendly smiles on their faces. Nyerrah was right. Her father was only too happy to act as chauffeur to the Shadow Man museum. Lisa, Wiz, the Count, and I hopped into the back row of the van, while Fist and Arnold hopped into the second row. Nyerrah sat in front with her parents. We stopped for breakfast at a nice restaurant along the way, but I had trouble eating. How could I think about pancakes dripping with syrup when I'd soon be inside the Orlac mansion? I'd be close to the Shadow Man mask and ring, close to the very things I needed to end Orlac's reign of terror. Would I be able to smuggle those objects out of the museum without being caught? I would only be borrowing them, but the people running the museum wouldn't believe that if I were caught. Caught. I didn't want to think about that. One step at a time.

We pulled up in front of the Rondo Orlac house. Did I say house? Try depressing, larger-than-life mansion, like something you'd find in a *Nightmare on Elm Street* movie. Two stories, jutting towers, shingled roof, over-size shuttered windows that looked like cold, black eyes. The whole thing gave me the creeps. Rondo Orlac really had taken his horror movie life-style seriously.

The red dice in my pocket turned over as we found a parking spot, and then they started popping like fire-crackers the closer we marched to the front door.

"What's that funny noise?" Lisa asked, craning her head around.

Think fast, Drac. "Oh, uh, a bad habit of mine," I improvised quickly, yanking at my fingers, "cracking my knuckles."

Lisa made a face but bought it. Talking and laughing, the nine of us crowded inside a hallway full of other Shadow Man fans. A smiling caretaker greeted us and began taking money. Nyerrah's father offered to treat us all, but he had already paid for breakfast, and besides, we all had healthy allowances. When we had all gotten our tickets, we moved into a side room to discuss who was going to do what. There were lots of things to do in the museum. Most of my friends signed up for the guided tour, but Nyerrah chose to see a movie about Rondo Orlac with her parents. That left me free to roam through the rooms at my own pace. Of course, security guards kept an eye on things, and I still couldn't figure out how I was going to "borrow" the mask and the ring. But I had faith in my Mandori abilities. The answer, the magic, would come to me.

Blending in with a group of chattering tourists, I moved slowly through a front room plastered with Shadow Man posters and paintings, then into a study filled with props and costumes from the very first Shadow Man films. Mannequins dressed as Shadow Man and assorted villains were posed in front of large film stills from the movies. All very fascinating, but not what I was looking for. Then, walking alone into the third room, I hit the jackpot.

I also hit a major snag.

There, in a large glass case, was exactly what I needed, the very mask and ring Rondo Orlac had worn as Shadow Man. There were also pages of his script, as well as framed fan letters from *Dracula* and *Frankenstein* stars Bela Lugosi and Boris Karloff.

I zeroed in on the ring and mask. Either one would be right for the shadow ceremony. Together they would be unbeatable. But how could I get my hands on them? The case was locked, and a dour-faced guard was standing only a few feet away. He eyed me now with a trace of suspicion as I pressed right up to the glass.

"Careful," he warned. "Too close and you trigger the alarm."

Terrific. Not only was the case locked, but it had an alarm. I'd never break in. Feeling a crawly sensation, I raised my eyes to discover Rondo Orlac laughing at me. It wasn't the ghost, but a large oil portrait of him that hung high on the wall against a purple velvet backdrop. The actor's eyes were staring directly at mine, his lip curled in a sneer, as if to say, I dare you to take what is mine. I dare you to try to win.

Squirming slightly under his gaze, but determined to go for it, I tried to remember Mandori spells that had to do with unlocking things or opening closed doors. Hard enough to think of the words with a guard standing a mere five feet away, impossible when the guided tour marched into the room, with Lisa waving and calling my name.

I needed to be alone. I needed to think in a quiet atmosphere. I would never be able to open the case with a mob around, and certainly not with Lisa and the rest of the Fang Gang screaming and yelling at me. I was going to fail. I was going to lose this round to Rondo Orlac unless something magical happened.

And then, incredibly enough, something did.

Hawk flew into the room, squeaking and diving at the heads of the people on the tour. There was instant chaos and screaming.

"That bird stole my hair bow!" exclaimed one girl.

"He got my postcards!" shouted a man.

"Catch him!" cried someone else.

Hawk winked at me before zooming out the door, objects dangling from his beak. An angry, noisy mob stormed after him. In a matter of seconds the room had completely emptied. Even the dour guard had left his post to follow the action. My pet pigeon had disobeyed my orders and followed me to the museum, but how could I be angry with him? He had saved the day. I turned my attention to the mask and ring lying in the glass case. What I needed was so close and yet impossible to reach.

I tried a Mandori trick. I shut my eyes and pictured a blank piece of paper. Very slowly words began to appear on the page. I held trembling hands a foot or so above the locked case and said softly: "Under cover, under glass, open to me in a flash!"

I raised my hands, and as I did, the lock silently turned and the lid slid open. I stared at the mask and ring for a second before reaching in to draw them out, and—

The alarm went off.

10

A shrieking sound filled the small room, and red lights flashed overhead in a control box. I stood frozen. Should I return the items, shut the lid? Or keep the mask and ring and try to run for the door and hope no one would catch me? Burglary was *not* what I had in mind when I went to H.O.W.L. High only three weeks ago.

I heard footsteps down the hall.

What should I do? Rondo Orlac was strong, but he had to be stopped. Not only for my sake, but for the safety of the Fang Gang. The evil shadow had played no favorites on Thursday when it decided to pay us a visit at school. That time it had come to scare us. Next time it might do something worse. On that sobering note, I made up my mind and thrust the mask and ring inside my pants pocket. I turned and was halfway to the door when Lisa burst in.

"What's going on?" she demanded. "There are guards heading for this room!"

I still had time to escape. I tried to take Lisa's arm to pull her out with me, but Miss Bossy wouldn't budge. She turned and spotted the open case and her eyes widened.

"No wonder the alarm went off!" she exclaimed. "The lid's up! I can fix that."

"Lisa, don't get near that thing!"

She broke free, not listening to me—as usual—and ran to the case. Just then I heard upraised voices and footsteps at the door. I was trapped. We both were trapped. No fair letting Lisa take the blame. I prepared myself for the worst as three guards dashed into the room.

"All right, what's going on?" one demanded, staring at me. The others hurried to the case. Lisa turned and gave everyone a big angelic smile.

"Why, nothing's wrong. See, I really *love* Shadow Man and I've seen all his movies and I guess I got too close to the glass or something to get a better look at his ring when the alarm went off."

The three men grunted and examined the case. I stood in miserable silence, waiting to hear, "Hey! The mask and the ring are missing! Arrest these kids!"

No one said anything.

One of the guards actually grinned at Lisa. "Another Shadow Man nut, just like my granddaughter. You did get too close, young lady. All right, Jim, turn off the system and let's go. We still got that darned bird to catch." The guards left after shutting off the alarm.

Didn't they see that the mask and ring were missing?

What was going on? I nervously edged over to Lisa, who was pointing to the case.

"Look, Drac, isn't Shadow Man's ring perfecta-mundo? And I love his mask!"

"What are you talking about?" I started to say when I followed the direction of her finger and did a double take.

The lid was closed, and the Shadow Man ring and mask were still there.

But that was impossible. Unless—

My Mandori spell had somehow substituted exact copies of the two items so I wouldn't be caught. Illusion, solid objects, whatever they were, the mask and ring looked perfectly real.

I stood a little straighter. Maybe I wasn't such a wimp warlock after all.

Everyone talked a lot in the van going back.

Everyone except Lisa and me.

She sat beside me, staring out the window the entire time—that is, when she wasn't turning around to give me these questioning little looks. I made a face at her once, to get her to laugh, but she just jangled her bracelets as if to say, Leave me alone. So I did just that. I left her alone.

When we arrived at school, we piled out of the van and thanked Nyerrah's parents, who had been terrific. Then everyone split in different directions. Most of the gang went in to have lunch, but Lisa decided to work on the Shadow Man script, and I ran up to my room. I had to hide the mask and ring. I really hadn't had time to study them carefully, but now I admired the detailed *S* and lightning bolt in the fancy silver ring and the iridescent black and purple mask. Reluctantly I put the items with *The Book of Shadows* and then started when I heard a tapping on the window.

Hawk was waiting for me, pecking impatiently at the glass.

"You did a great job today," I praised him as I let him in. "Just don't let it go to your swollen pigeon head."

In all the excitement of the morning I had forgotten Uncle Frederico, but now I realized that I wanted to talk to him. He knew all about Rondo Orlac and the shadow and could probably tell me something about the ceremony I had witnessed in the actor's private theater. I looked at my watch. Nearly noon. No time now to call. I had to meet my stunt coach. Later, right before dinner, I'd call Uncle Freddy.

For the next few hours I worked in the gym, rehearsing my jump as Shadow Man until everyone felt certain I knew what to do. I practiced leaping off a specially designed ledge on to inflated air mattresses. Those same air mattresses would travel with me when I performed the jump at Specter Empire, but they wouldn't be placed at the bottom of the tower. Mr. Mendoza would put them on a special platform positioned about twenty feet below the tower ledge. Because I wouldn't be falling too great a distance, I wouldn't need to wear a bulky shoulder harness or cord attached to my waist. If Rondo Orlac hadn't gotten so obsessed with believing he was really Shadow Man, he probably would have taken the same safety precautions and lived to finish *Revenge of Shadow Man* and many other sequels.

As soon as I finished rehearsing, I hurried back to the dorm to see if the book, mask, and ring were still safely hidden. They were. Hawk made sure of that. He strutted in front of the closet like a guard, and I patted his feathers and praised him. Then I grabbed some change and went to call Uncle Frederico. Only this time I decided to use the one in the lobby. The brightly lit, always crowded lobby. No harm in avoiding any menacing shadows until I knew what I was doing.

Uncle Freddy was in and listened in silence to my entire adventure. When I told him I had the Shadow Man mask and ring, he embarrassed me with his praise.

"If you had any doubts before about your abilities as a warlock, nephew, you shouldn't have now. It takes an extraordinary amount of skill to collect items belonging to a ghost, a very active ghost, I might add. And to steal them right under his nose, in his very own house—" Uncle Freddy chuckled, then grew serious. "Orlac's going to come after you to get those things back. You must fool him and attack first."

I swallowed. "You mean, perform the shadow ceremony?"

"Exactly. As soon as possible—tonight if you can. You know what to do—you have the spell memorized. There is nothing I can tell you that you don't already know."

"But where do I hold the ceremony? And, Uncle Frederico, what do I do with the shadow after I call it forth?"

"The best place to hold the ceremony is in the same

99

spot the actor held his, but that's the museum and you can't do that. You can perform it anywhere, basically, as long as it's in the lowest level of a building." My uncle was silent for a moment, then sighed. "As to your other question, nephew, I can't answer. You will face the shadow, and at that moment you will know what to do. Just remember how well you did at the Orlac estate this morning. You've got what it takes to face the ghost of Rondo Orlac—or his shadow. I have faith in you as a Mandori."

My uncle said a few more comforting words, then hung up.

That very night. The shadow ceremony would be that very night.

Somehow I got through dinner and the agonizing hours until it grew dark. During that time I mapped out my plan. I took a piece of paper and listed every single thing I could remember from the scene in the underground theater. I wrote down Orlac's clothes, the candle, a midnight blue handkerchief, and the Shadow Man mask and ring. I borrowed the items I needed from the costume and special-effects department. By the time lights-out was called, I was all set.

And so was my pigeon.

Hawk knew what I had planned and wanted to go with me. I started to say no, and then changed my mind. A fourteen-year-old klutz warlock (although I could sense the klutziness was changing) needed all the help he could get in a late-night scary ceremony. So the pigeon went under one arm, and the bag containing *The Book of Shadows* and all the other items went under the other.

As silently as possible, I crept down the back stairs to the service elevator in the kitchen. Everything was deserted and quiet at ten o'clock at night—except for the pounding of my heart and the clicking of my dice.

Hawk pecked furiously at my arm.

"Yes," I told him, "we *have* to use the basement. I don't like it any more than you do. Now, I'm counting on you for moral support, so don't get all nervous on me!"

The elevator doors slid open. Hawk made low squeaking noises as we stepped inside and pushed the button to descend—down to the very bottom of the school. I had been there once before and couldn't get out fast enough. The basement of H.O.W.L. High was dark and creepy, filled with clammy tunnels and twisty passages. And who knew what else?

Hawk stiffened as the elevator shuddered to a stop and the doors opened.

"Just remember how well we did at the Orlac museum this morning," I said in a low voice as we stepped out. "We're unbeatable."

Was I saying that to make me or Hawk less afraid? Who knew? The fact is it seemed to help us both. My pigeon ruffled his feathers, as if to say, I'm ready for anything that ghost can dish out. Lead the way.

Lead the way? I'd like to, but where? I stood in a dimly lit gray cement passage and stared at all the tunnels leading off from it. While I hesitated, I shivered and pulled my jacket tight around me. Even Hawk seemed to feel the cold. Farther along I could hear the faint sound of the furnace, thumping like the heartbeat of a giant creature.

But right then a heartbeat sounded comforting to me. I wasn't sure if this was another Mandori "nudge" or not, but I decided to go with it. I motioned to Hawk. We turned left, my pigeon perched on my shoulder, and walked along a narrow cement tunnel with pipes hanging overhead. The closer we got to the furnace, the heavier the pounding. Or was that my heart?

Without warning Hawk took off and headed for a large doorway a few feet down the tunnel. Grumbling under my breath, I followed the pigeon inside a pitch-black room. I groped for a light switch near the door, and when I saw where Hawk had led me, realized it was the perfect spot to hold the shadow ceremony. I wasn't the only one to get these Mandori magic nudges! I was standing in a large, almost circular room with dozens of empty clothes racks.

"Must have been used for costume storage," I said to Hawk. "It's perfect for the spell."

I put the bag on a nearby table and began to remove the clothes racks from along the back wall. As I worked, Hawk nervously circled the room, as if to keep the evil spirits away.

Nice try, I thought as I finished my task, but pigeon power alone wouldn't stop the ghost or his shadow from appearing.

Cut it out, I ordered myself. Don't even think about that awful hissing *thing*. If I pictured it too clearly, I might not be able to go through with the ceremony, which is just what Rondo Orlac wanted. Well, Orlac was in for a surprise that night because I wasn't going to back down. As if sensing my determination, Hawk stopped flying around the room and landed at my feet.

I leaned down and stroked him. "Are you ready? Ready to face the shadow?"

He peered up at me with a steely glint in those beady eyes. I had my answer.

"Good, because I'm ready, too."

I opened the bag and pulled out the extra-large midnight blue handkerchief dotted with stars and triangles. I flapped it in front of Hawk.

"This will be the center of my circle of power," I explained. Hawk pecked at the cloth. "Correction—*our* circle of power."

Taking the bag, I moved to a spot about twenty feet from the wall and placed the handkerchief a foot in front of me on the floor. Then I rummaged in the bag and pulled out a fat purple candle. This I placed a foot behind me. Then I fished out a small packet of herbs (borrowed from the school kitchen) and put them and a book of matches next to the candle.

It was time to begin.

Trying to quiet my trembling fingers, I dipped my hand into the bag and took out the purple and black Shadow Man mask. I held it in front of me. In as strong a voice as I could produce, I said,

"Mandori I am,
Mandori I'll remain,
But with this mask,
I take Rondo Orlac's name."

On went the mask. Next, the ring. It had appeared so large in the display case, but now it would fit my finger perfectly. I held it out in front of me and said,

"Mandori I am,
Mandori I'll remain
As I put on this ring,
I put on Rondo Orlac's name."

Did I imagine it, or did my hand tingle as if from an electrical charge when I slipped the ring on?

The atmosphere in the room changed. Before, it had been damp, cool, and empty—just an old space used to house actors' costumes. Now the room seemed to be waiting for something, holding its breath. The pounding of the furnace faded. The giant heartbeat slowed—and then stopped. I was completely alone in the basement, cut off from all my friends, in what felt like an underground tomb now.

The silence scared me.

And then I felt something behind me. A presence, watching me. Something dark and cold.

I turned around.

Nothing was there. Yet I still felt eyes on me. Staring. Stone-cold eyes.

I was shaking now. Could I go through with the spell after all? Would the ghost of Rondo Orlac be too strong a match for me? What did I know as a magician? I was a kid. I wasn't even a full Mandori. I was half-human, and that human half was terrified right then.

I stared down at Hawk, who had sensed my fear. Suddenly words my uncle once said popped into my mind: "Good magic doesn't need big weapons to fight bad magic. The right words, the right attitude, will."

If anyone qualified for the Bad Magic award, it was the ghost of Rondo Orlac. I might not be one hundred percent Mandori, but perhaps the half that was could battle Orlac with good magic and win.

Ignoring my fear, I continued my ceremony. I lit the purple candle, sprinkling herbs on it to make the flame catch and burn in bright rainbow colors. Now came the difficult part. The lights had to be turned off.

I motioned to Hawk. "The light switch, please," I ordered.

The pigeon hesitated, then did as commanded. One tap of his beak and the entire room was plunged into darkness.

Shivering, feeling that invisible presence gaining substance behind me, I waited while the candle burned. The light it threw picked up my silhouette and made a shadow against the back wall. As the flame burned brighter, the shadow grew larger.

I picked up *The Book of Shadows* in my trembling hand and said:

"Shadow of Orlac,
I command thee,
Come to your master,
and obey me."

Complete silence except for the sputtering of the candle and the thudding of my heart. I threw more herbs on the flame and repeated the spell.

"Shadow of Orlac,
I command thee,
Come to your master,
and obey me."

Everything was still, yet I felt a draft. The shadow on the wall stretched and expanded and rose so that it almost touched the ceiling. A shape stirred in its depths, a shape far different from mine.

And now the draft became a chilly breath.

Something was in the room with me.

Trying to control my fear, I repeated the words, standing and speaking as much like Rondo Orlac as I could to trick the shadow. Icy currents swirled around me, making the flame flicker and almost die. Slowly, as in a nightmare, I heard a soft hiss coming from the wall. It sounded like a snake, ready to strike—or a shadow about to appear.

"Shadow of Orlac," I said in a firm voice and thrust *The Book of Shadows* in front of me. "I command thee—"

I got no further than this when the twisted black shape took on a life of its own and slid across the ground toward me.

It all happened so fast I couldn't run or turn away. The twisted black mass stopped in front of me and grew right before my eyes. The shadow turned and stretched, taking on one shape after another. It rose a foot in the air, then two, then three, four, five. It billowed out in all directions like a giant octopus, or some nightmare monster, with many hands reaching out. There was a dark mist surrounding the shadow, a mist smelling like something locked away in a damp cellar for years and years. The *thing* grew bigger, until it topped six feet. The horrible black stumps for hands clawed out in my direction. When I looked into its center, something I had never done before, I could make out the outlines of a face. A monster face, with coal red eyes, lumps of skin for a nose, and lips the color and shape of worms.

The lips opened now. The shadow leaned closer. I could feel its chilly breath on my face and smell that foul odor.

"What do you command, master?"

I had been so frightened that I forgot to tell the shadow what I wanted him to do, perhaps the most important part of the entire ceremony. Without saying the command, the shadow might simply do whatever it wished, and that might include devouring me.

I swallowed nervously and held *The Book of Shadows* up.

"Shadow of Orlac, I command thee, untie this knot and then you go free."

Before I could move, the huge monstrous being slid closer. Its hands rubbed against the tiny book and accidentally touched mine. They were cold and rough and unpleasantly wet, like the tentacles of an octopus. I shivered as the hands fell away. The red knot was untied. The shadow had obeyed me!

Without warning, however, the six-foot being began to slide over me, around me, behind me. I was being crushed by an ice-cold shadow. I couldn't breathe. I couldn't see. The dark, foul-smelling mist pressed against me. I struggled, but my arms were pinned by the force of the being.

"And then you go free!" I yelled, gasping for air. "Go free!"

As soon as the shadow touched my ring, the ring of Shadow Man, it drew back. The being had been cold, but when it brushed against the ring, it hissed and sizzled like a lit match falling into a patch of snow. With a shriek the shadow twisted itself into a hurricane force that rushed into the flame of the candle. As soon as it completely disappeared, the flickering flame went out.

Total darkness engulfed me. The shadow was gone. I was alone except for my pet pigeon.

Immediately the furnace kicked back into life, creating that comforting heartbeat sound.

"Hawk?" I whispered. "Are you all right?"

My pigeon made some cooing noises, then flew over and flicked on the light. I stared around the room, blinking at the wall in disbelief. Had I really called forth Orlac's shadow and then sent him away? Had I, Dragomir Johnson, done all that?

Hawk circled my head and landed happily on my shoulder. He leaned down and pecked at the tiny *Book of Shadows* in my hand.

I pulled off the Shadow Man mask and ring and touched the book. "We did it, Hawk, we did it. The Book of Shadows is open to me now, and that means I can find the spell to destroy Rondo Orlac."

I had won a major battle against the evil ghost.

One battle alone did not mean the entire war, however.

I knew that Rondo Orlac would find me soon and fight back.

"

I wasn't afraid anymore.

The following Wednesday I sat outside in the courtyard for my special-effects class and didn't once worry about the shadows surrounding me. It felt good to be able to concentrate on my studies or my Shadow Man script without always looking over my shoulder.

Now I paid full attention to Wiz, who was standing before the class with a gun in his hand.

"All right, freeze!" he snarled at the man facing him. "One more step and I shoot."

Mrs. Kreighley and the rest of the Fang Gang watched this tense scene without moving a muscle or blinking an eye.

"I warned you!" said Wiz when the man moved. He raised the gun and fired. Bang! Bang, bang, bang, bang!

The man clutched at his stomach, his face in agony. A row of bullet holes popped up on his shirt, creating an all-too-gory and bloody mess. He staggered over to where I sat, rolled his eyes, and fell heavily to the ground, gasping his last breath.

He didn't really die, because he hadn't even been wounded. Wiz had used a cap gun for this staged stunt for our special-effects class, and the kids loved it, cheering and clapping. The "dead" man, Bob Wheeler, a respected stuntman with a long list of film credits in action movies and horror films, jumped nimbly to his feet, to explain how the shooting was achieved.

"All stunt work is dangerous to some degree," he said, "so you have to protect yourself very carefully. When you're doing a shooting scene, you place a metal plate over the part of the body where the 'bullet' is supposed to hit—in this case, my stomach. Then a small explosive cap is placed on the plate, and for more realism you attach a sac of stage 'blood' over the cap, which is set off electrically by a battery."

The Count raised his hand. "What about jumping through windows? How do you smash through glass and not get hurt?"

Bob Wheeler grinned. "You just asked about a specialty of mine. In the film I'm doing now, I'm doubling for an actor playing the villain. In the last scene I have to leap through a plate-glass window twenty stories up and go flying through the air. In the old days we went through windows made of transparent sugar. But sugar windows melted under hot studio lights, so now they're made of a special plastic. It shatters in the same way as real glass, but without the sharp points that could really hurt someone."

"What do you land on?" Lisa asked.

"A whole bank of specially insulated airbags. And a lot of prayer. Let me give you one example. . . ."

Bob Wheeler proceeded to recount a story about a problem with one of his earliest leaps. All around me kids were scribbling notes or listening with rapt attention.

As fascinating as it all was, my attention wandered to the tiny *Book of Shadows* hidden beneath my notebook. I no longer had a shadow to worry about, but I did need to locate the right spell before Saturday, the anniversary of Rondo Orlac's last stunt. It sounded simple except for one thing: There were over two hundred spells in the book, and I had to read each one carefully to see if it was the one I wanted. It was taking me forever to creep through the list of short spells. I didn't have forever. I had until Saturday. That meant I was constantly studying the little book—when I wasn't memorizing my lines for the movie.

"Need any help?" Lisa whispered. She sat beside me on the grass, trying to peek behind my notebook where *The Book of Shadows* was hidden.

"Help in what?" I snapped, irritated at being caught.

"I don't know, you tell me. Something's got you going."

Her eyes caught mine and actually seemed to see beyond the mask I wore at school. But that was crazy, of course. Lisa had no idea I was half warlock or that Rondo Orlac was haunting me.

"You sure I can't help?" she asked in a soft voice.

At that moment I wished I could tell her everything, but I stopped myself. Ghosts, warlocks, shadows? Lisa would listen for one minute and then burst into laughter, thinking it was a joke.

Some joke, I thought glumly, realizing I had over one hundred more spells to read. Then Fist, who was sitting on my other side, accidentally bumped my arm. The notebook and the Book of Shadows rolled off my lap and onto the ground. Quick as a flash I reached for the Book of Shadows, but Lisa got there first. She flicked it open somewhere in the middle and stared at the words, meaningless to her, I was sure. Just terrific, I muttered to myself. Here come the one thousand and one questions from Miss Want-to-Know-It-All Horowitz.

But without a blink of surprise or curiosity, she handed the book back to me and then turned away to join in the discussion with Bob Wheeler. I was so startled by this lack of interest that I momentarily forgot about the book. Then I glanced down to the page Lisa had selected. The word *falcon* in big bold letters jumped out at me. Since falcon is a type of bird, I immediately thought of flying and Rondo Orlac's leap off the tower. Skimming the page hurriedly, I realized that I had found the spell he used!

Had I found it or had Lisa Horowitz?

I turned to stare at the dark-haired girl, a question niggling at my mind. Lately Lisa had been in all the right places at all the right times. She had loosened the red silk knot, served as my unwitting accomplice during the "break-in" at the Rondo Orlac estate, and now managed to put her hand on the very spell I desperately needed.

Was it coincidence? Luck?

Or something more?

No good brooding about that, I thought as the special-effects class broke up. I had to take off and start memorizing the spell. Before I got ten feet, though, something prompted me to glance back. Lisa was in line to talk to Bob Wheeler, but she was staring right straight at me. And there was an expression in her eyes I couldn't figure out.

Two days later, on Friday, the Fang Gang and I were at Specter Empire to rehearse for our Shadow Man movie. It was the first time we were allowed back on the set since that Saturday visit with the "Entertainment Now" crew. Now we had permission from Mr. Madrix to hold our final rehearsal there in front of cameras. Mrs. Kreighley and several security guards from the lot stood in the back of the Shadow Man interior set, patiently waiting for us to begin.

"All right, quiet," Wiz called, and everyone immediately stopped talking. In professional movie lingo we were doing a "take."

"Sound," he said next, and Arnold started the recorder.

"Speed," Arnold said when the tape was running smoothly.

"Camera," Wiz called and adjusted the Ikegami EC-35 video camera mounted on a Steadicam support.

"Rolling," he said next.

Nyerrah dashed before the camera in her Grecian robe costume and operated the clapperboard. "Scene three, take one."

"And . . . action!" Wiz cried.

Fist, dressed as the evil Galaxy Master Khan-Tong, but minus the dual heads for rehearsal, strode across his headquarters and stopped before an impressive-looking panel. Fiddling with some knobs, he said, "No one ever enters or leaves Apparition Castle without my knowing it. I know you're here, Shadow Man. And I shall find you. And when I do—"

He threw back his head and laughed and then shouted, "Guard!"

One of the extras hurried through the phony stone door into the chamber.

"Yes, Galaxy Master," he said, snapping to attention.

"Have your men bring my daughter up from the dungeon. It's time Ethera served her purpose as a decoy."

"Very good, Galaxy Master." The guard nodded and exited.

Beside me, Lisa, playing the part of Ethera, adjusted her cloak and fiddled with her hair.

"I'm on next," she whispered. "Wish me luck."

"Good luck, Ethera," I said.

She entered the scene, but minutes later Wiz screamed, "Cut!" There was going to be yet another delay, this one of a technical nature. It might take two minutes, it might take twenty. Time for me to brush up on the spell. I had memorized my Shadow Man lines, but I still had a way to go with the words in the spell in

The Book of Shadows. And the next noon I had to be letter perfect when I performed the stunt.

Sneaking a look around to be sure that no one was watching, I tiptoed off the Galaxy Master set and found a dimly lit spot way in the back. There was nothing there except for folding chairs, changes of costumes for the actors, and a floor-length wall mirror. Nice and peaceful and deserted. I leaned against one side of the mirror and pulled out the book to study.

Repeating the words of the spell over and over, I lost track of time until I sensed a movement behind me.

"Drac," a voice said in a low growl. "Dragomir Johnson."

The voice was dark and menacing—and all too familiar.

I clenched the pages of the book, trying hard to keep my hands from shaking.

"Turn around," the voice commanded.

Don't listen, I told myself. Just keep on reading. The words began to blur in front of my eyes. A curious kind of twilight darkness descended on the back of the set. I felt my resistance weakening. I felt eyes burning into the back of my head.

Very slowly I turned and—a hand shot out of the mirror and grabbed my arm!

Rondo Orlac glared at me in the glass, his angry face only inches from mine.

"How dare you steal my ring and mask?" he demanded. "How dare you take my shadow from me?"

I tried to squirm out of his grasp, but his fingers clung fiercely to my arm.

"I—I was only borrowing your ring and mask," I replied. "I'm going to return them to the estate."

"The same way you'll return my shadow, you liar?"

"That shadow was evil," I said with increasing anger. "You had no right to scare my friends that way."

The actor's dark eyebrows shot up. "I'll do more than scare your friends, Mandori. When I get you alone at the top of the tower tomorrow, I guarantee I'll put on a show they'll never forget."

I twisted in his grip. "You leave them out of this!"

He pulled me closer, spotting *The Book of Shadows* in my hand.

"Of course I'll leave them out of this, if you'll do one thing for me—give me back my book."

I shook my head. "It's not your book. It never was your book. It belongs to my family, and it's going to stay in my family."

A sneer appeared on the actor's lips. "Such brave words. We'll see how brave you are tomorrow without your uncle to hold your hand. I still have power at Specter Empire."

He gave my arm a shake, and I cried out. Losing my temper, I blurted out, "You won't have it after I repeat the spell you used for your last stunt twenty-five years ago. I can banish you with that spell!"

The rage in Rondo Orlac's eyes changed to panic. His fingers loosened and let go of me. I jumped away, rubbing my arm.

You shouldn't have told him, you shouldn't have told him, my mind repeated, but it was too late.

"Well, we'll just have to see about that, won't we?" His

voice had become quiet and ominous. "We'll just see if you can banish me from this studio. You will *never* play Shadow Man in a movie, my friend, and I will prove that to you tomorrow. So go right ahead and learn those lines of the spell. I'm not frightened. I am Shadow Man, and I have the powers to win."

Did he? I didn't know how.

But I would find out the next day at twelve noon.

12

Saturday, October 1.

We were all on location at Specter Empire to shoot our film.

I squinted at my watch under my Shadow Man cape: 11:55 A.M. Then I looked up at the cold stone tower. In five minutes I would need to jump off that high ledge and pray I'd remember every single word of the spell Rondo Orlac had used twenty-five years earlier.

And if I couldn't? I shivered slightly in the sunshine, wondering what unpleasant tricks the ghost would have in store for me and the Fang Gang.

"Hey, Shadow Man, daydreaming again?" Wiz called from behind his camera.

"Give the guy a break," the Count said. "If you had to take a flying leap off a building and dive twenty feet, you'd want to be somewhere else, too!"

119

Lisa came up beside me. "Are you worried about the stunt, Drac?"

"That's the easy part."

She gave me one of her concerned looks. "What's the hard part?"

"Getting my lines straight."

"But, Drac, there are no lines in this scene," she called as I walked to the door of the tower. Behind me Mr. Mendoza and his crew were frantically locking the huge safety crane into place and adjusting the insulated air mattresses. At least I didn't need to think about the stunt. The special ledge would safely break my fall.

But what about Rondo Orlac? Would I have to worry about him?

I entered the cool tower and began to climb the circular stairs. All the night before I had replayed his challenging words. "So go right ahead and learn those lines of the spell. I am Shadow Man, and I have the powers to win."

Was he bluffing? So far I hadn't received a visit or a vision from the ghost, and that bothered me more than anything else. What was he waiting for? I climbed steadily upward, growing more and more nervous as I neared the top.

Don't think about Rondo Orlac. Think about the spell. Think about how great it's going to feel winning the filmmaking competition with the Fang Gang. Think about—

"Leaving so soon and not stopping to say goodbye?"

His face was a ghostly blur in the shadows. He stood between me and the door to the tower ledge. If he didn't move or I couldn't push past him, I'd miss my twelve noon deadline.

"Let me through," I said.

He smiled, his eyes glittering in the dark. "Oh, am I stopping you? How rude of me! Please, allow me to get the door for you."

What game was he playing now? What was going on? The ghost actually unlatched the door and swung it open, allowing sunlight to stream through the murky interior. Wherever light touched his body, Rondo Orlac became invisible.

I swallowed and squeezed past, then glanced at my watch. Eleven fifty-seven. Three minutes and counting.

I turned back. The door was still open. I couldn't see Rondo Orlac in the sunshine, but I could hear him.

"Did you think I'd allow you to stand up here and take over my role as Shadow Man? Did you think you could actually perform my stunt and repeat the spell I used so many years ago? You will *never* get that far because you won't remember the spell. You won't remember a word."

"I will!" I protested. "I can say it in my sleep!"

The ghost clapped his hands and said a strange word. Out of the doorway flew the red silk cord, only this time it whipped around my right wrist and tied itself into a tight knot. I tried to pull the strands apart but couldn't. It dug into my wrist.

"Hey!" I shouted. "This hurts!"

"A small price to pay for your vanity in thinking you could beat me. Just try to repeat the spell now!"

I raced over to the edge of the tower and peered down,

past the bulky safety crane. My friends were lined up behind Wiz, the trusty cameraman. They gave a cheer when they saw me.

"Good luck, Shadow Man!" Fist cried.

"Break a leg!" shouted Arnold, who was promptly nudged by the Count.

"What a stupid thing to say to someone diving off a tower!"

"Ready to roll when you are, Shadow Man!" instructed Wiz.

I wanted to laugh, but I was too scared. Just get a grip on yourself, Drac. Of course you know the spell. You know it inside out, backward and forward. Why, the first line is—

My mind was blank.

I couldn't remember a word!

Of course I knew the spell. But my memory refused to cooperate. What was wrong with me? As if on cue, the silk cord twitched playfully against my skin. I stared down at it in horror.

The cord had to be cut. I'd never remember a word unless the knot came off my wrist. But scissors and knives didn't work against this type of magic. Only shadows could, and I wasn't about to play with that particular brand of fire again.

Besides, it was nearly twelve o'clock. One minute left. If I had *The Book of Shadows* with me, I could read the spell, but I had left the book in my dorm room with instructions for Hawk to guard it with his life.

I was going to fail. The ghost had tricked me. There was nothing I could do except perform the stunt and hope and pray Rondo Orlac didn't have anything more up his sleeve as I tumbled through the air.

I stood at the edge of the tower, giving Wiz the signal. Forty seconds to go, thirty-five, thirty.

I screwed up my courage—it was now or never—when the tower door burst open. Lisa raced over to me.

"Wait, Drac, don't jump! Wiz sent me up here to have you remove that red cord from your wrist. It's showing up too clearly in the telephoto lens."

Without thinking, I blurted out, "It won't come off, Lisa. I can't get it undone."

"Well, maybe I can."

From beneath the folds of her costume, Lisa produced a pair of scissors, just an everyday, slightly tarnished, grade-school pair of scissors. But when she touched the tips to the red silk cord, the sunlight struck the dull surface like a bolt of lightning. The knot wriggled against her fingers and then, incredibly, amazingly, split apart.

At that magic moment three things happened at once: The words to the spell popped clearly back into my mind, I stepped to the edge and opened up my cape as a signal to Wiz to start rolling, and the ghost of Rondo Orlac came rushing at me from behind in blind fury.

We fell off the ledge together.

In slow, extra-slow motion, we dived into the air, our purple and black capes billowing like two kites tangled up together. I was in another time, another dimension. Seconds felt like minutes as I repeated the spell exactly as it was written in *The Book of Shadows*. Beside me a panic-stricken Rondo Orlac kept trying to claw at my cape. As we somersaulted against the sky, I knew the ghost wanted to drag me down with him, to whatever new place he'd be calling home.

He didn't get his wish. The last word of the spell flew out of my mouth as I landed with a soft thump on the air mattresses. The ghost of Rondo Orlac gave me one last anguished look as he went soaring past, his cape swirling a final goodbye before he disappeared at the very bottom of the tower.

"Cut and print!" Wiz exclaimed. "That's a take!"

Beside him all my friends were jumping up and down and cheering.

I goggled at them stupidly from my perch on the air mattress. Had I really lifted the curse of Shadow Man? Was Rondo Orlac gone forever? In minutes Mr. Mendoza lowered the crane and had me on the ground. I was surrounded by the Fang Gang. But there was something I had to do. Someone I had to see. Excusing myself, I ran back up to the top of the tower.

Lisa was leaning against the roof, waiting for me, the scissors still in her hand.

I took a deep breath and looked at her.

"Where did you get those scissors?"

She gave an embarrassed laugh. "These old things? They've been in my family for years."

"They're *yours?*" That piece of information startled me more than anything else I had heard or experienced over the last four weeks. How could Lisa own magic scissors? Unless—

She gave me a half-defiant, half-searching look from out of those light green eyes. No one said a word. And then the pieces of the puzzle slid into place, and I knew about Lisa Horowitz and her strange behavior.

Both of us leaned forward at the same time.

"You're a witch," I said.

"You're a warlock," she replied.

"Well, only half," I admitted. "On my mother's side."

"I'm only half as well," she echoed. "On my father's side."

Her face scrunched up as she said the words, yet she appeared relieved and almost happy to be sharing her secret. Exactly the same way I must have looked.

"How did you figure out I was a warlock?"

My puzzled face made her smile. "I've known since I saw the video you did of your going-away party. Your relatives look a lot like mine."

"But why didn't you say something? Why didn't you tell me?"

"And let on I was a witch, too?" She shook her head, lifted her chin. "No, I'd never let on, especially since I knew you were trying to keep that side of yourself hidden. So I did what I do best and pretended we were both normal."

I laughed aloud. "That's why you kept staring at me. I wondered about that." I remembered the funny looks she had given me on the way home from the Rondo Orlac estate.

The Rondo Orlac estate! I jumped up and snapped my fingers.

"You were the one who got that lid closed when the alarm went off!" My happiness faded suddenly. My face fell. "Did you substitute the fake mask and ring? And here I thought I was being such a hotshot magical genius!"

"I only closed the case," she said. "You did all the rest."

"Really?" My Mandori ego shot up twenty feet. "Are you sure?"

"I'm sure."

"But you found the spell in *The Book of Shadows* for me, admit it! And you even loosened the knot, remember?"

She grinned at me from beneath her bangs. "I loosened it a little bit with some of my own magic, but I never could have gotten it completely undone. And as for the spell, you would have found it in time yourself. I just wanted to speed up the process."

"You did, Lisa. You really helped. You practically saved my life with those magic scissors." I paused, light dawning. "Did you know the whole time about Rondo Orlac haunting me? Could you see him, too?"

"He never appeared to anyone except you, Drac, but I knew you had seen him on that first visit to Specter Empire. That's why I kept watching you. I was worried that the ghost might hurt you."

I walked over to the ledge and looked down. There was nothing to see at the base of the tower. No cape, no shadow, no evidence of Rondo Orlac. I closed my eyes and listened. Listened with my Mandori sense of hearing. No whispers, no rustling sounds, no spooky laughter.

126

"He's gone, Lisa," I said, turning around. "The ghost of Shadow Man is really gone."

"But the live Shadow Man is still here, right in front of me, and he's going to make a great one. Except . . ."

Her voice dwindled off. She cocked her head to one side and examined me like a painting in a modern art museum.

"Except what?"

"Well, would you mind a few acting suggestions? I've got several ideas you might be able to use."

I rolled my eyes. Miss Know-It-All Horowitz hadn't changed one bit.

Somehow, though, it didn't bother me as much.

I couldn't believe it, but I had found a real friend in Lisa.

13

The awards presentation for the Horror Junior Filmmakers Competition was scheduled for Halloween night.
And H.O.W.L. High had been personally invited to
attend.

The Fang Gang was in heaven. *The Revenge of Shadow
Man* was one of five other entries up for first place. The
kids at school treated us like celebrities, and we had even
been interviewed by a news station. Any connection to
Rondo Orlac and his unfortunate tragedy twenty-five
years earlier was still a big draw.

"You filmed on the Specter Empire backlot and
worked from the original movie set?" the plump, dark-
haired interviewer had asked, thrusting her microphone
in front of my face. "Were you a victim of the ghost that
supposedly haunts anyone daring to play the Shadow
Man role?"

I hesitated and then caught Lisa's eye. She made a face and winked at me.

"That's just a silly rumor," I said lightly and grinned at the woman. "And you can quote me on that."

The night of the event two huge limousines pulled up to the school, extended super-deluxe ones with tinted glass, television sets, stereos, and enough room for a football team to shower and change in after a Super Bowl game. Dressed to the teeth in our best clothes, the Fang Gang scrambled to the luxurious seats and nervously talked about the awards ceremony all the way to the Hollywood Bowl. Dukes Madrix rode in our car, and Coretta Kreighley and several other teachers rode in the other. I was too nervous to be cowed by the presence of the bristling principal that night. All I kept thinking about was the Mandori clan.

After Lisa and I confided in each other about our witch and warlock status, we decided to go one step further and invite our families to the ceremony. "Sort of like a coming-out party?" I had joked at the time with Lisa. But now it didn't seem like such a joke. It was one thing to talk to a fellow witch about blending in with all-human kids, but quite another to introduce Aunt Tagoor and Cousin Wa'albi to school friends. Both Lisa and I agonized over the decision but finally mailed the engraved invitations off to our respective households. Both had called to confirm. Now I was biting my nails over the outcome. Beside me Lisa gently tapped my arm. "It'll turn out fine," she reassured me. "You'll see."

I knew what *I* would see all right, but what about Wiz and the Count and Nyerrah and Mr. Madrix and everyone else at the Hollywood Bowl? What they'd see would be quite a shock.

Would I ever live this evening down?

The limo swung on to Hollywood Bowl Road, and all the kids cheered. Talk about a classy place to view our films! Mercedes, Rolls-Royces, Porsches in gleaming black and silver purred along beside us. Valets jumped to attention as movie stars stepped out and were immediately snapped by the press.

My heart sank even lower. Photographers would have a field day with the Mandori mugs.

Excitement flared all around us, but major fireworks were going off in my stomach. Our limos pulled up at the gate a distance from the Bowl, and everyone eagerly tumbled out, except me. Thank goodness no photographers bothered to take our pictures. Dukes Madrix gathered us all together and counted heads as well as tickets. It was a madhouse, and for a second I hoped I wouldn't be able to find my family. But then the crest of Uncle Frederico's dark hair popped into view, and right next to him was a neon-pink aura floating above Aunt Tagoor, flanked by my solid-looking father and my mother dressed in her colorful silver-glitter scarves and beads. Tubby Cousin Wa'albi sported his special glasses with enlarged middle frame for his third eye and Uncle Idoor brought up the rear like a character out of Frankenstein's laboratory. Circling overhead, my favorite pigeon emitted hawk battle cries. Just your average, everyday American family and house pet.

But, hey! They were my family and not a bad bunch of relatives at that.

My face broke into a huge grin as I waved my hand to catch their attention and then turned to the Fang Gang.

"Quit your jabbering and pointing out stars. I want you to meet some *real* stars right now. Everybody, this is my family, the Johnson and Mandori tribe . . ."

There was a split second of startled silence as the kids got an eyeful of Dragomir Johnson's loved ones.

"Did he say his *family?*" came the whispers behind my back.

"Why, they look like—like—"

"Very *spirited* people!" Lisa chimed in nicely.

"And *super,* too!" I added. As in *super*natural!

My mother bent over and kissed me. My father hugged me. Uncle Frederico gave me a wink to imply we shared a mighty big secret. The aunts and uncles and cousins proclaimed how happy and proud they were to be in Hollywood on Halloween, viewing a film of mine. In absolute silence the H.O.W.L. High kids stared at us and then Wiz snapped his fingers in triumph.

"Now I know who you are and why you look so familiar! You're the geniuses who were in that video, the going-away party for Drac!"

"That's us!" Aunt Tagoor beamed, her pinkish aura turning red with pleasure.

"Boy oh boy oh boy, do I have questions for you—for all of you," began Wiz, putting a comradely arm around Wa'albi's shoulders. "You see, I'm a director and . . ." He led my cousin away, chatting a mile a minute.

"This is exciting!" Nyerrah exclaimed, gazing at Aunt Tagoor in awe. "I've never met a real, well, witch before."

And pretty soon the "supernatural" side of my family was hot and heavy into conversation with the non-supernatural side of my friends. Lisa's folks hadn't shown yet, but when they did, we knew we had nothing to worry about.

Mr. Hackerdorf sidled up next to me and watched the proceedings with pursed lips. "What did Nyerrah call your aunt just now? A witch? Well, if that doesn't take the cake, the cake, the *cake!*"

My mother turned her beautiful but stormy green-gold eyes on him.

"You don't believe in witches, Mr. Hackerdorf?"

"No, I don't, it's absurd, but—how did you know my name?" He raised an eyebrow and sniffed. "Anyway, the whole business of magic is just so much mumbo jumbo. Why, if you're a witch," he glared at my mother, "then I'm a toad."

We left Mr. Hackerdorf squatting on the ground, deep green cheeks puffed out, croaking his indignation.

About the Author

Bubble, bubble, toil and trouble . . . Ellen Leroe has loved cooking up tales of mystery and magic ever since she wrote her first book, *Skull and Dagger Island,* when she was nine years old. She has authored novels for teenagers and younger readers featuring her favorite subjects: poltergeists, ghosts, and cupids—not to mention a mean mechanical robot.

Born in East Orange, New Jersey, she now lives in San Francisco, California, where she enjoys views of the Bay Bridge and Alcatraz Prison. She has no plans to move, although the earth moves her quite often, the latest experience being the 7.1 earthquake in 1989.

She gets many of her ideas for her books from the diaries she wrote from the fifth grade all the way through college. Other inspirations come from her niece and two nephews, who live close by and read all her stories.

In addition to writing, Ms. Leroe reads books (about four a week), and especially loves those she calls "high on the Creepmeter of Scare." She has traveled all over Europe and now enjoys aerobics, conversation with good friends at local coffee shops, and the theater—and a good horror movie or two.